Computer Classics ®

The Ram Of God

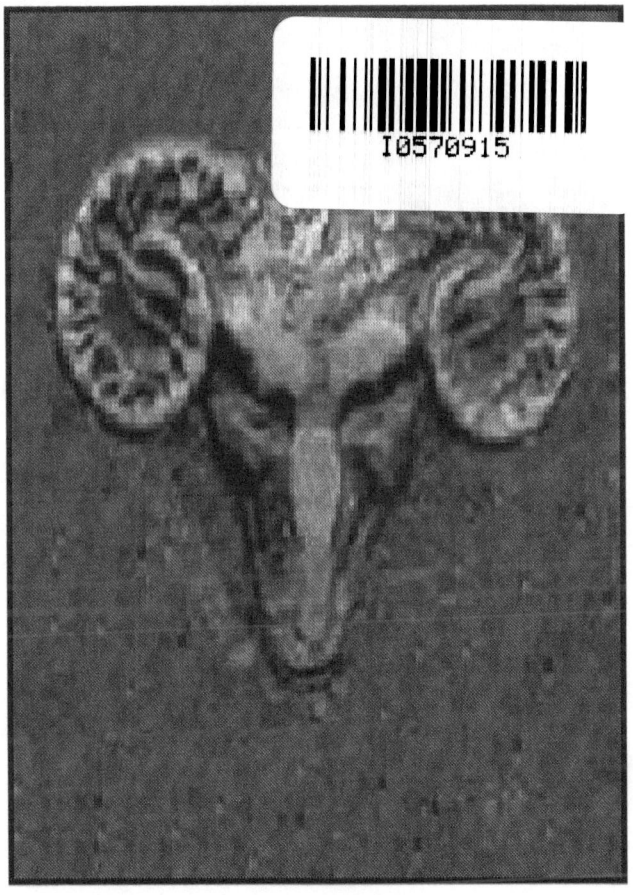

I0570915

Edward Ronny Arnold

The Ram of God is based on the Bantu legend of
the Beberu Munga - Ram of God

The Ram of God
Published By
Computer Classics ®
497 Elysian Fields Road A-11
Nashville, Tennessee 37211

The Ram of God © is published in e-book format by Computer Classics ® on the Computer Classics ® website www.computer-classics.com.

Library of Congress Control Number: 2003096517

ISBN: 0-9721216-7-6

Printed in the United States of America

The Ram of God
Contents

THE HERULI   5

THE ANGEL JAYKAL   13

THE BANTU   19

DAY ONE   26

DAY TWO - THE ISLAND OF GOD   30

THE PLOT TO MURDER THE ANGEL JAYKAL   33

DAY THREE - THE MUTINY   36

DAY FOUR - THE FEAST TO GOD   51

GOD HEALS THE BANTU CHILD   53

GOD DESTROYS THE MAN HEALER IN FIRE   56

GOD HEALS THE BANTU VILLAGE   58

THE RAM OF GOD   60

GOD'S WARRIORS   63

THE BEBERU MUNGA   67

GOD HEALS THE LIONS   72

THE WATER OF PEACE   76

ONE YEAR LATER   79

The Ram of God

ONE MONTH LATER   82

THE BANTU LEGEND OF THE "BEBERU MUNGA"   85

THE BANTU LEGEND OF THE "MWANA POZA"   89

APPENDIX   91

THE AUTHOR   99

The Heruli

The young girl walked on the docks of Pylos. Behind her, her mother and father followed closely. She walked to the far end and she stopped. She turned to her mother and father. "It is here," she said. "It is here we will wait."

They stood at one of the docks. There were many docks and small ships were at them. This dock was empty. All around them people were busy. The fishermen had returned with the day's catch. Men, women, and children were busy sorting the fish and placing the fish in straw baskets. The baskets of fish would be taken to market where they would be sold.

No one noticed the young girl and her parents at the empty dock. The people were busy preparing the day's catch.

The sun was high as the young girl and her parents stood at the empty dock. They did not speak to each other or to anyone. The three people stood at the empty dock. They looked outward toward the sea.

Near the three people, a man surveyed his catch. There were many fish. He placed them in straw baskets and he moved the baskets from his small ship to the dock. The fisherman bent downward to pickup one of the baskets. As he stood, he looked outward toward the sea.

He saw it!

Quickly approaching the docks was a ship. The ship was a war galley. The sail was full as the ship quickly approached. The man looked at the sail. The sail bore the head of a ram.

The Ram of God

The fisherman dropped the basket in his hand. "Look! Look!" the man, yelled. Many people looked towards him. He pointed outward toward the sea.

Many people heard his cry and they looked toward the sea. They saw the warship. The people looked at the sail. A large animal head was on the sail. It was a ram.

"Heruli!" one man yelled.

The people began to scream and run. They dropped what they held in their hands and they ran. They dropped their baskets and their fish. Men, women, and children ran. They ran away from the docks. They left everything. They ran for their lives.

The docks were quickly empty of people.

The docks were empty except for the three people. The three people did not run. They waited for the Heruli warship to dock.

The warship quickly approached the Greek port of Pylos. The commander ordered the sail lowered. Many crewmen ran about the warship. They released the sail ropes and the sail was quickly lowered. Then, wooden oars appeared from the sides of the ship.

At the rear of the warship was a large drum. One of the crew stood by the drum. The order to beat the drum was given.

Boom! Boom! Boom! Boom!

The crewman beat the drum at a slow, steady pace. The wooden oars moved at the speed of the drum. Many oars dipped deep into the azure Greek waters.

The oars did not move forward, the oars moved backward to slow the warship.

The Heruli warship began to slow. The oars slowed the ship.

Boom! Boom! Boom! Boom!

The crewman stopped beating the drum and the wooden oars stopped moving. They remained in the water. The oars slowed the warship. The ship moved very slowly as the wooden oars were pulled inward. Slowly, the war galley approached the empty dock. Then, several crewmen jumped from the warship. They carried large ropes and they quickly tied the ropes to large wooden poles.

The warship bumped against the dock and tugged against the large ropes. Then, the ship stopped. The crewmen quickly climbed onboard the warship.

The crewmen ran about the deck yelling orders to prepare to leave the ship. Several of the crewmen carried a long wooden plank to the edge of the warship and they pushed the wooden plank toward the edge. The plank fell heavily on the dock. It bridged the edge of the ship and the dock.

The young girl stood at the dock. When the wooden plank was placed, she began to walk on it. She walked on the plank toward the ship.

She was to board the Heruli warship.

One of the crewmen yelled at her, "Stop!"

The young girl stopped. She looked at the crewman. He was Heruli. The Herulis and Goths invaded Athens many years ago. The Herulis defeated Emporer Romulus Augustulus at Ravenna two years earlier. The Heruli roamed the seas at will. They pillaged and plundered cities.

The Heruli followed no leader. They followed no God. They lived only to conquer. They were the most feared of any soldier.

Roman soldiers were afraid of them.

The crewman was dirty and unkempt. He wore a tunic of animal fur. On his chest was a breastplate. The breastplate bore the symbol of the Heruli, the ram.

"Stop!" he commanded.

The young girl looked at the crewman. "Who is your captain?" she asked.

The crewman drew his sword and he held it up. "Move!" he commanded.

The young girl did not move. Her mother and her father, who waited with her, walked quickly on the wooden plank towards her and they stopped behind her. The three people stood before the Heruli crewman who held a sword in his hand.

"Who is your captain?" the young girl asked.

Several of the crewmen approached the plank. They drew their swords. One of the crewmen stepped forward, "Move!" he said.

"Move away from the plank. We must leave the ship for supplies," he added.

"You will not leave this ship!" the young girl commanded.

The crewmen began to laugh at the young girl. She was but eight years of age. They looked at her clothing. Her clothing was simple, a long white robe. She was Greek. She had long black hair that was braided and she was thin. The man and women were young. They were also dressed simply and they were Greek.

The crewman walked on the plank towards the dock. The young girl did not move. He approached the young girl and he held his sword up to frighten her. The young girl was not frightened.

"You will not leave this ship!" she commanded.

"Stop!" a voice called from the ship. The voice was the commander of the Heruli warship.

The commander walked towards the wooden plank.

"Move!" he commanded.

"If you do not move, we will kill you!" he added.

"There is one on your ship I must see!" the young girl replied.

"There is no one on this ship that you know!" the commander replied.

"There are many in the hold of your ship. I have been sent to one of them," the young girl said.

The commander and the crewmen looked at each other. They were shaken. No one knew of the people in the hold.

The Ram of God

"There are no people in our hold," the commander replied.

"There are many in the hold of your ship. They are Bantu. I have been sent to one of them," the young girl said.

The commander and the crewmen looked at each other. They were shaken. No one knew of the people in the hold of their ship. They looked at each other. 'How did this young girl know of the people in the hold,' they thought.

The commander looked at the young girl. He was puzzled. "Who sends you? Odoacer?" the commander asked.

"God!" the young girl replied.

The crewmen were puzzled. They looked at the young girl. "What God?" the commander asked.

"There is only one God! The God of Abraham and the God of Moses! There is only one Messiah, Jesus Christ!" the young girl said.

The crewmen began to laugh. "She is a Christian," one of the crewmen said.

The crewmen laughed.

"Who are you? What does God want you to do?" the commander asked.

"My name is Theophilia. God has sent me to one on this ship. You will not leave this ship! You will return these people from where they came!" Theophilia said.

The Ram of God

The crewmen stopped laughing. The commander looked at the young girl. "Move!" he commanded.

Theophilia did not move. She was not afraid of the Heruli.

"You will not leave this ship! You will return these people from where they came!" Theophilia commanded.

The commander raised his sword. The crewmen near the plank raised their swords.

Theophilia looked at the Heruli. She was not afraid of them. "You will not leave this ship! You will return these people from where they came!" Theophilia commanded.

The commander was angered. "Who commands us to return these people?" he asked.

"God commands you return these people from where they came!" Theophilia answered.

"We follow no Christian God. We do not follow Odoacer. We will not return these people!" the commander said.

"You defy God?" Theophila asked.

"We follow no God!" the commander responded.

"If you do not return these people of your own will, God will send a great warrior to return them," Theophilia said.

"We will not return them!" the commander said.

"So be it!" Theophilia replied.

The Ram of God

The commander moved toward Theophilia. He held his sword upward as to strike her. Theophilia did not move. The commander looked into her eyes. She was not afraid of him. Her eyes did not show fear or anger.

They stood on the wooden plank. The young girl stood with her mother and her father behind her. The commander stood in front of her. He held his sword as to strike her and she would not move. Many of the Heruli crewmen stood behind the commander and they held their swords upward.

The commander stared into Theophilia's eyes. She was not afraid of him.

"It is done!" Theophilia said.

The commander was startled by her words. "What is done?" the commander asked.

"You defied God's command. God sends a great warrior to return these people from where they came. You will not leave this ship!" Theophilia said.

The commander began to laugh. He turned to his crewmen. "The God of the Christians sends a great warrior to battle the Heruli!" the commander said.

The crewmen laughed.

The commander turned and he pointed his sword toward Theophilia's father. "Is it you?" the commander asked.

"This man is my father. God did not send him to battle," Theophili said.

The crewmen laughed.

The commander pointed his sword toward Theophilia's mother. "Is it you?" the commander asked.

"This woman is my mother. God did not send her to battle," Theophilia said.

The crewmen laughed.

The commander pointed his sword toward Theophilia. "Then it is you!" he said.

The crewmen laughed.

The commander looked at Theophilia. "We defeated the legions of Romulus. The Romans run from us and the Goths fear us. Your God sends a young girl to battle us. What God is this? What God has no soldiers but young children to do battle for him?" the commander asked.

The Angel Jaykal

"God did not send me to battle. God sent me to one on this ship. God sent me to deliver his command," Theophilia replied.

"If your God did not send you to battle the Heruli, who does your God send to battle us?" the commander asked.

Theophilia raised her hand. She pointed her hand toward the commander. Then, she slowly moved her hand toward the end of the warship. She pointed her hand toward the large drum.

Theophilia looked toward the end of the warship. She looked toward the large drum.

"God sends him!" she answered.

The commander and the crewmen looked towards the back of the warship. They looked towards the drum. They gasped.

Beside the drum stood a soldier. He was large. His hair was dark black and his beard was dark black. Upon his head was a helmet of gold. They looked to his chest. Upon his chest was a breastplate. The breastplate was made of gold. They looked at the hilt of his sword. The hilt of his sword was made of gold. The soldier held no shield. His arms were folded before his chest.

The soldier stood by the drum. He did not move. He did not speak.

"Where did he come from?" one of the crewmen asked.

"How did he get onboard the ship?" one of the crewmen asked.

"He is not Roman!" one of the crewmen said.

"He is not Greek!" one of the crewmen said.

"Look at his breastplate, it's gold!" one of the crewmen, said.

"Who is he?" several of the crewmen asked.

The commander turned to Theophilia. "Who is this man?" he asked.

"Before you is the angel Jaykal. God sends the angel Jaykal to return these people from where they came," Theophilia said.

The Ram of God

"Your God sends a angel to battle us?" the commander asked.

"God sends the angel Jaykal to return these people from where they came. You will not leave this ship! You will not harm the Bantu! If you defy God's commands, the angel Jaykal will destroy you," Theophilia said.

The commander looked at the angel Jaykal and then he turned towards Theophilia.

"No man can defeat the angel of God. No army can defeat the angel of God. The angel of God commands the fire of God," she added.

The commander turned to his men. "Kill him!" he ordered.

Several of the crewmen began to move toward the angel Jaykal. They held their swords and they were to charge him. Suddenly, the angel Jaykal appeared before them. In his hand he held his sword. The sword was of silver with a gold hilt. The blade of the silver sword burned in white fire. Swiftly, the angel Jaykal struck each man with his sword of white fire. When the sword struck the men, they became as of fire. The fire consumed them.

As quickly as the angel Jaykal appeared before the crewmen, he disappeared.

"Where did he go?" one crewman asked.

Several of the crewmen pointed toward the drum. "He is there!" they said.

The crewmen looked toward the drum. The angel Jaykal stood beside the drum. "No!" one of the crewmen said. "I have been watching him! He did not move!"

The crewmen were afraid. Many moved away from the angel Jaykal. They moved to the far end of the ship. The crewmen looked at the angel Jaykal. They were afraid of him.

The commander stood on the wooden plank. Many of his crewmen stood behind him and they held their swords. The crewmen stood to prevent Theophilia from boarding their warship.

The commander was afraid. "What is this?" he asked.

"You defied God's command. God has sent the angel Jaykal to return these people from where they came. God has sent me to one on this ship," Theophilia said.

"Take me below! Take me to the people you have on this ship!" she commanded.

The commander was afraid. He could not speak.

"God sends me to one on this ship! Take me to the people on this ship! If you do not take me below, I will go alone!" she commanded.

The commander was afraid. He could not speak.

Theophilia yelled, "I will board this ship! You will not stop me!"

The commander was afraid. He could not speak.

Theophilia screamed, "I will board this ship! The angel Jaykal will battle before me!"

The Ram of God

The commander was frightened. He looked to the angel Jaykal and he looked at Theophilia.

Suddenly, the angel Jaykal was before Theohilia. In his hand he held the silver sword. The blade of the sword burned in white fire. The angel Jaykal began to walk forward on the wooden plank.

Quickly, two Heruli crewmen pushed before the commander. They stood on the wooden plank and they held their swords to strike the angel Jaykal.

The angel Jaykal stepped forward and he struck the two crewmen with his sword. When the sword touched them, the two crewmen became as of fire. The fire consumed them.

Many of the Heruli crewmen yelled. They pushed their way before the commander. They charged the angel Jaykal.

The angel Jaykal continued to walk forward. As the crewman approached him, he struck the Heruli crewmen with his sword. When the sword of white fire struck them, they became as of fire. The fire consumed them.

The commander watched the angel Jaykal battle before Theophilia. As the angel Jaykal moved forward, Theophilia followed.

He watched in terror, as his men were defeated.

The angel Jaykal's sword was swift. His crewmen did not strike one blow against him. When the sword of white touched them, they became as of fire. The fire quickly covered their bodies. Then, they were gone.

The Ram of God

The fire of God consumed them.

The Heruli crewmen watched their kinsmen defeated in battle. They began to scream and yell in fear. They turned and ran from the wooden plank. When they ran, they pushed the commander from the wooden plank. They pushed the commander to the deck of the ship. They ran towards the far end of the ship.

The angel Jaykal walked forward on the wooden plank. He was to board the ship. In his hand he held his sword. The silver blade burned in white fire.

The angel Jaykal walked to the end of the wooden plank and he stepped onto the deck.

Theophilia followed the angel Jaykal up the wooden plank. She stood on the edge before the ship and the angel Jaykal stood on the ship. The commander stood alone before the angel Jaykal.

All of his crewmen ran to the far end of the ship. The angel Jaykal held his sword of white fire in the air as to strike the commander. The commander dropped his sword and he quickly fell to his knees. As quickly as the angel Jaykal appeared, he disappeared.

Theophilia stepped from the wooden plank onto the ship.

"What is this? What soldier does God possess?" the commander asked.

Theohilia did not speak. Slowly, the commander stood. He looked toward the drum. The angel Jaykal stood beside the drum. He did not move or speak. The commander looked to the far end of the ship. All of his men were there. They were afraid of the angel Jaykal.

"Take me below! Take me to the Bantu!" Theophilia commanded.

The Bantu

The commander stood and he motioned for Theophilia to follow him. Theophilia turned to her mother and father. "I will go alone," she said. "Return to the dock."

Theophilia's mother and father turned. They walked on the plank to the dock. They stood and waited for her.

The commander walked to a large wooden hatch in the ship. He lifted the hatch and a rush of stale air came upward. The air had the smell of urine and human refuse. There was a ladder that led downward. Theophilia held to the ladder and she descended. The commander followed her.

The first hold of the ship was dark. There was a small oil lamp. Light came from the holes in the ship where the wooden oars rested. Near the sides of the war ship were many Bantu men. The men were chained. They held to the wooden oars. Theophilia looked at the men. There were marks of a whip upon their arms, legs, and backs. They had been beaten.

She looked at their bodies. The Bantu men were very thin. They had not eaten. The Bantu men looked at her. Their faces were blank.

Theophilia spoke to the men. She spoke in their language. "God has not abandoned you! God heard your prayers!"

The Ram of God

"God has delivered you!"

The Bantu men gasped. The young girl spoke to them in their language. They had prayed to God to help them. They had prayed to God to free them. The young girl told them God heard their prayers.

The Bantu men began to speak among themselves.

There were several crewmen near the Bantu men. The crewmen held whips. Theophilia looked to the men. "Release them!" she commanded.

The commander looked to the men. He nodded his head to release them.

"No!" one of the crewmen said. The crewman lifted his whip. "Quite!" he yelled. He was to strike one of the Bantu men when the angel Jaykal appeared before him. The crewman gasped when he saw the angel Jaykal. The angel Jaykal held his sword. The sword was of silver with a gold hilt. The sword burned in white fire. The white fire lit the entire hold of the ship.

The Bantu men held their hands before their faces. The white fire burned bright and the white fire hurt their eyes. Near the Bantu men were large casks. The casks held gold and bronze items. The gold and bronze reflected the light from the burning sword. The casks held stolen items.

The angel Jaykal held his sword to strike the crewman with the whip.

The crewman slowly lowered his whip. The angel Jaykal stood with his sword of fire held in the air. The crewman was afraid. He dropped the whip. As suddenly as the angel Jaykal appeared, he disappeared. The commander and the crewman rushed up the ladder to the deck of the warship.

"Where is he? Where is he?" the commander yelled.

"He is there!" many of the crewmen yelled.

The crewmen were at the far end of the warship. The angel Jaykal was at the other end. The angel Jaykal stood by the drum. The angel Jaykal did not move or speak.

"He was below!" the commander yelled.

"He has not moved!" many of the crewmen yelled.

The commander ran towards the door to the hold. He quickly went down the ladder. "What is this?" the commander asked Theophilia.

"These people are protected by God! You will not harm them!" Theophilia said.

"How is this possible?" the commander asked.

"Release them!" Theophilia commanded.

The Bantu men were released from their chains. Theophila walked to each one. She spoke very gently and she touched them. "God heard your prayers. God will heal your wounds."

When she touched them, God healed them.

The commander looked to the Bantu men. There were many marks of the whip on their backs, legs, and arms. When the young girl touched them, the marks of the whip were gone.

The Ram of God

Theophilia turned to the commander. "Take me to the others!" Theophilia commanded.

The Heruli war ship had two levels. The commander led Theophilia to a wooden hatch in the floor. When he opened the hatch, the smell of human excrement was horrible. A wooden ladder led downward. Theophila went down the ladder. The commander followed Theophilia.

The hold was full of women and children. There were many young men who were ill. There were no old men or women. All of the Bantu were young. The Heruli had captured the people to be sold as slaves. The Heruli had placed as many young men, women, and children as possible on the war ship.

Theophilia turned to the commander. "This is not a travesty of man, this is a travesty to God!" she said.

Theophilia spoke to the Bantu in their language. "God has heard your prayers. God has sent the angel Jaykal to return you to your home."

The Bantu men and women turned towards Theophila. She spoke their language.

"Among you is one whom God will bless! Among you is one who will do God's will," Theophilia added.

The Bantu men and women looked at Theophilia.

Theophilia began to walk among the Bantu men, women, and children. There were many that were ill. She went to them and she touched them very gently. As she touched them, God healed them.

The Ram of God

She came to a young woman who held a child. The child was a male. He was one year of age and he was crying. The young boy was very ill. Theophilia did not touch him. She walked past the woman and the child.

Theophila touched all of the Bantu men, women, and children that were ill. She then returned to the one child she had not touched. She took the child from his mother's arms. The young boy cried. Theophilia whispered in the child's ear and the child stopped crying.

Theophilia turned to the Bantu men, women, and children. She spoke in their language. "The power of God has healed this child!"

"When I was a young child, I was very ill. God sent a young girl to me. This girl was blessed. God healed through her hands. When she touched me, God healed me. The gift God gave to her, God took from her. God gave the gift to me. God heals through my hands."

"It is time to pass the gift of God to another."

Theophilia passed her hand over the child. She again spoke to the Bantu men, women, and children in their language. "It is the will of God that generations to come will know the power of God through the hands of a child. What was given to me has been taken from me. What has been taken from me has been given to this child. God will heal no other through my hands. God will heal through the hands of this child."

Theophilia looked upward. She turned to the Bantu men, women, and children and she said, "This child is protected by God himself. No man, woman, child, or beast of the earth shall harm this child. This is God's will. This is God's command."

Theophilia returned the child to his mother. "What name have you given your son?" she asked.

The Bantu woman responded, "His name is Habib."

Theophilia spoke very softly. "Your child will serve God. Return to your place and share the blessing God has given."

Habib's mother began to cry. She held to Habib and she wept. Theophilia placed her hand gently upon her shoulder. "Do not be afraid. Habib's father, your husband, is safe. He will be returned to you," Theophilia said.

Habib's mother looked upward towards Theophilia. She began to smile.

Theophila turned to the Bantu. She spoke in their language. "Do not be afraid! You are all safe! God protects you! These men will not harm you! The angel Jaykal will return you to your home."

The commander was unnerved. He had not seen such a thing. The young girl healed all that she touched.

"Give them food and water!" Theophilia commanded.

The commander motioned for the Bantu to be given food and water.

Theophilia climbed up the ladder to the first level. She looked at the Bantu men. She spoke to them in their language. "You are safe! God heard your prayers! God has given to you a great blessing! His name is Habib! He will lead you to God! He will lead you to Jesus!"

The Bantu men nodded their heads.

Theophilia climbed the ladder to the upper deck of the war ship. She walked towards the wooden plank and she walked across the plank to the dock.

The commander followed her to the edge of the wooden plank. He remained on the ship.

Theophilia turned towards the commander. "The angel Jaykal will return these people from where they came. God will provide all you need."

"We have no food! We have no water!" the commander said.

"God will provide all you need," Theophilia said.

"Who will man the oars? Who will man the sails?" the commander asked.

"The angel Jaykal commands this ship! There is no need of oars or wind," Theophilia said.

"The sea? The sea is dangerous! We can not return!" the commander said.

"The angel Jaykal commands this ship! God protects these people," Theophilia said.

"In three days, your crewmen will rebel. You must stop them! If you do not stop them, the angel Jaykal will destroy them!" Theophilia added.

"How will I stop them?" the commander asked.

"Pray to God! God will show you the way!" Theophilia said.

POP! SNAP! KAPLUP!

The ropes holding the warship broke loose. The warship moved away from the dock and the wooden plank dropped into the ocean. The war ship moved. It slowly moved away from the dock. The warship moved away from the dock and turned toward open sea.

The crewmen were afraid. The warship moved without oars or sail. The warship moved toward the open sea at a very fast pace. It quickly passed the ships in Pylos. The warship headed toward open sea. The warship traveled where they had came.

Day One

The Heruli warship moved quickly on the sea. It headed southeast towards the end of the great land. The warship moved quickly in the still Greek waters.

The crewmen and the commander were afraid. They were on the far end of the ship away from the angel Jaykal. The angel Jaykal stood beside the large drum. He did not move or speak.

The crewmen looked at the water. The sea was calm. They held their hands in the air. There was no wind yet the warship moved with a speed greater than any sail. The calm waters parted as the warship moved quickly.

The warship had been traveling for several hours. Then, the hold of the ship slowly opened. A Bantu man came slowly came up the ladder. He walked carefully to the deck of the ship.

The Bantu man looked to rear of the warship. He saw the angel Jaykal standing near the drum. The Bantu man knelled onto the deck and he lowered his head toward the angel Jaykal. The angel Jaykal lowered his head toward the Bantu man.

The Bantu man lowered his head toward the angel Jaykal.

The angel Jaykal spoke in the language of the Bantu. "You are free! God has sent me to return you from where you came!"

The Heruli commander and the crewmen were afraid. They watched the Bantu man bow to the angel Jaykal and the angel Jaykal bowed his head to the Bantu man. The angel Jaykal spoke to the Bantu man. They did not understand what was said.

The angel Jaykal spoke again. "Rise! You are no longer slave! These men are not your master! These men will not harm you!"

The Bantu man slowly rose. He turned toward the hold of the ship and he quickly spoke. "Unkulunkulv Kaga" - *The creator protects us*.

Slowly, many Bantu men came from the hold of the ship. They walked toward the first Bantu man and they knelled before the angel Jaykal. Then, women and children emerged from the hold. The Bantu gathered on the deck of the ship. They knelled before the angel Jaykal.

The Bantu began to speak. "Munga Kaga" - *God protect us*.

The Ram of God

The angel Jaykal spoke, "Rise! You are no longer slave."

The Bantu began to shout and cheer. They stood and they began to dance with excitement. The men began to shout. They pointed toward the angel Jaykal, "Vita Munga kaga moto upanga!" - *War God protects us with fire sword.*

The Bantu men jumped and yelled. "Vita Munga pigana kaga mtumwa!" - *The war God fights to protect slaves.*

The women and children laughed. They hug one another. They were free! The God of Abraham and Moses heard their prayers. God sent the angel Jaykal to free them and to return them to their home.

The Heruli commander and the crewmen were frightened. They watched the Bantu dance and laugh. The commander looked to his men. They were frightened. He had never seen his men afraid. They fought the Romans and the Goths. None of his men cowered before the enemy. This was different. This man, this angel of God, was an enemy unlike any other. The angel of God moved with great speed and his sword of fire consumed all it touched.

The angel of God did not come to battle them. He came to return the Bantu.

They looked to the drum. The angel of God stood by the drum. He did not move or speak. The Heruli looked to the sea. The sea was calm. There were no waves. They held their hands upward. There was no wind. The warship moved quickly trough the calm sea. The warship moved quicker than with sail.

"How can this be?" many of the Heruli asked.

The Ram of God

"Is there a God?" many of the Heruli crewmen, asked.

The Bantu shouted and danced for many hours. The angel Jaykal did not move or speak. The Bantu men yelled. "Kula samaki!" - *Eat fish*. The women and children yelled in excitement. The Bantu men ran to the first hold of the ship and they quickly returned with fish and water. Quickly, the food was eaten. Quickly, the water was drunk.

"We have no food! They have eaten it all!" one of the Heruli crewmen said.

"We have no water!" many of the Heruli crewmen said.

"We will starve and die of thirst!" many of the Heruli crewmen said.

The Heruli were afraid to move. They huddled together in fear of the angel Jaykal.

The sun set and the night sky was filled with bright stars. The stars lit up the ship and the calm sea. After many hours, the Bantu fell asleep on the deck of the warship. After many hours, the Heruli crewmen fell asleep. The warship continued to move swiftly through the calm sea.

The angel Jaykal stood by the drum. He did not move or speak.

Day Two - The Island of God

The Heruli crewmen were awakened by the sound of the warship resting on sand. The warship came to a slow stop. They jumped upward when they heard the sound of birds.

It was morning and the sun was slowly rising. The warship had stopped. The warship was resting on a sand bar. Not far from the ship was an island.

"Where are we?" many of the Heruli crewmen asked.

There was an island. It was beautiful. There were large coconut trees and many bushes bearing fruit. Near the beach was a small waterfall. The waterfall poured fresh water into the sea.

"Where are we?" many of the Heruli crewmen asked. They looked at each other. They had never seen or heard of this island.

"This island is on no map!" one of the Heruli crewmen said. "I have traveled these waters for many years. There is no island!"

The Heruli quickly stood. They looked toward the drum. The angel Jaykal stood near the drum. He was not asleep. He did not move or speak.

On the beach was much laughter. The Heruli crewmen turned to look at the island. The Bantu men, women, and children had left the war ship. They ran in the sea and played on the beach. Near the beach were their water casks. The Bantu men had filled them. Near the water casks were baskets of fresh fruit. The women and children had gathered fruit from the trees and filled the baskets.

The Heruli were afraid. They did not know what this was.

Two Bantu women climbed aboard the ship. They held a basket of fruit and a small cask of water. The two women slowly approached the Heruli. They offered the fruit and water to the Heruli. One of the Bantu women spoke to the Heruli. "Kula kande maji." - *Eat food and drink water for the journey.*

The Heruli crewmen did not accept the food.

Suddenly, one of the Heruli crewmen yelled. Two of the crewmen had drawn their swords and they ran towards the angel Jaykal. The angel Jaykal was before them. In his hand was his sword. The sword burned with white fire. The two crewmen were consumed in the fire when the angel Jaykal's sword struck them.

As quickly as the angel Jaykal struck the crewmen with his sword, he disappeared.

"Where did he go?" many of the crewmen asked.

"He is there!" one of the crewmen yelled.

The angel Jaykal stood beside the drum. He did not move or speak.

"What is this?" the commander asked. "He did not move! I saw him strike the two men with his sword of fire!"

The crewmen were afraid. They moved as close to the end of the war ship as they could.

The Ram of God

"Run!" one of the crewmen, yelled.

The crewman jumped off the edge of the war ship into the sea. He quickly ran through the surf to the sand. As he emerged from the water, the angel Jaykal stood before him. The angel Jaykal held his sword in his hand. The sword burned in white fire. The sword moved swiftly. The crewman was consumed.

As quickly as the angel Jaykal appeared before the crewmen, he disappeared.

"Where is he?" many of the Heruli asked. They turned toward the drum. The angel Jaykal stood beside the drum. He did not move or speak.

The Heruli were afraid. The angel Jaykal was in more than one place at one time.

The Bantu men, women, and children witnessed the crewmen consumed in fire. They quickly fell to their knees on the sand beach and they bowed toward the angel Jaykal. They began to shout.

"Vita Munga fisha Huruli!" - *War God put to death Hurli.*

"Uchaji Munga!" - *We are afraid of God.*

"Mjakazi mtwana mwana mtumwa Munga!" - *Women, men, children slaves to God.*

The Bantu men, women, and children bowed on the sand. They were afraid of the angel Jaykal.

The angel Jaykal stood by the large drum. He turned toward the Bantu kneeling in the sand and he spoke in the language of the Bantu. "Do not be afraid of God! Do not be afraid of me! God will not harm you! I will not harm you! Rise! You are no longer slave!"

The Bantu slowly rose to their feet. The men placed the casks of water and the baskets of fruit onto the warship. The Bantu men helped the women and children to board. When the last Bantu had boarded the warship, the ship moved.

The warship slowly moved from the sand bar. Slowly the ship turned toward the sea. Quickly, the warship headed southeast. The warship moved quickly. The sea was calm. There was no wind.

The Plot to Murder the Angel Jaykal

The Heruli crewmen gathered together. "We must kill him!" one of the crewmen said. "He can not kill all of us!" he added.

"We must act together! " one of the crewmen, said.

"No!" the commander said. "We can not defeat him. Truly, he is the angel of God!"

"No! He is but a man. There is no God! There are no angels! It is a trick!" one of the crewmen said.

"He has killed twelve of us! His sword burns in fire and the crewmen became as fire when he struck them." one of the crewmen said.

"We have not seen him fight! He is but a man!" one of the crewmen said.

"No! He is an angel of God! No man fights as he fights," the commander said.

The Ram of God

The Heruli crewmen looked towards the angel Jaykal. They turned to each other and they lowered their heads.

"I will kill him! I will strike him dead with my bow!" one of the crewmen said.

The crewmen looked at the one who spoke. In his hands he held his bow. He held an arrow with a metal tip. "If his breastplate is made of gold it will be soft. This arrow will pierce his armor and his heart. When he is dead, we will hang him from the mast and return the slaves to Pylos," the one crewmen said.

"Shield me so he can not see me draw my bow," the crewman with bow said.

The Heruli crewmen nodded their heads. They stood in front of the one with the bow. The crewmen stood in front to hide him. They looked to the drum. The angel Jaykal stood beside the drum. He did not move or speak.

The crewmen, with the bow, placed the arrow. He moved towards the side of the warship. There were many in front of him. He slowly raised his bow.

Suddenly, the angel Jaykal was before him. In his hand he held his sword. The silver blade burned in white fire. The blow was swift. It cut through the body of the crewman. The crewman was cut in half. Both pieces burned in white fire. The crewman was consumed in white fire.

A quickly as he appeared, the angel Jaykal disappeared.

The crewmen began to yell. The commander was standing watching the angel Jaykal. The angel Jaykal did not move or speak. The commander turned to where the crewman, with the bow, had stood. There was nothing.

"What happened?" the commander asked.

"The man! The angel of God slew him!" several of the Heruli crewmen said.

"No!" the commander said. "He has not moved! I watched him!"

"He is dead! The angel of God slew him. The fire of the sword consumed him!" one of the crewmen said.

"The blow cut him in half! The two half's burned in white fire!" one of the crewmen yelled.

"The white fire consumed everything! His bow is gone! He is gone!" one of the crewmen yelled.

The Heruli crewmen were afraid. They ran to the hatch of the war ship and they entered the first level. The commander did not run to the hatch. He stood near the end of the ship. He watched the angel Jaykal.

'How can this be!' he thought. 'Is there a God?' he asked himself.

The Bantu men, women, and children stood on the deck. They bowed to the angel Jaykal. The commander stood, alone, on the far end of the ship. He watched the angel Jaykal.

'Is there a God?' he asked himself again.

The commander looked toward the angel Jaykal. The angel Jaykal looked toward the commander. "Yes!" the angel Jaykal said.

The commander fell to his knees before the angel Jaykal. He lowered his head. The angel Jaykal lowered his head toward the commander.

The commander buried his head in his hands. "What have I done? What have I done to these people?" he wept.

The commander looked upwards and he clasped his hands. "Forgive me!" he pleaded.

The Bantu watched the commander weep. They became very quiet and they sat down upon the deck of the ship. They did not speak. They watched the commander weep. The commander asked God to forgive him.

Day Three - The Mutiny

The Heruli crewmen huddled together in the first level. The first level was dark. Only one oil lamp was lit. The crewmen lit many lamps. They were afraid. They were afraid of the angel of God.

The day passed slowly. The night passed slower. Many sounds came from the deck of the war ship. The Bantu were laughing and dancing. In the early morning, the sounds stopped. The Bantu slept on the cool deck of the war ship. The Heruli sat in the hot hold of the first level.

"It is us who are the slave! The Bantu are the masters!" one of the crewmen said.

"Yes!" many of the crewmen replied.

"The Christians sacrificed many to their God. Perhaps the angel is waiting for a sacrifice," one of the crewmen said.

The Ram of God

"Yes! A sacrifice!" many said.

"It is the commander who has brought this upon us. It is the commander who spoke to the young girl. The commander wants the treasure and to sell the slaves," one of the crewmen said.

"Yes!" many answered.

"We will sacrifice the commander. When the angel leaves, we will return to Pylos," one of the crewmen said.

"The treasure!" one of the crewmen said. "We will offer the treasure!"

"Yes! We will offer the treasure to the angel of God. We will sacrifice the commander. When the angel leaves, we will return to Pylos," one of the crewmen said.

"Yes!" many, said.

The sun was rising as the Heruli crewmen began to bring the treasure from the first hold of the ship. There were many casks of gold and silver. There were vases of copper and statues of gold. The Heruli had looted many cities near Greece. They had looted Athens itself.

The commander was standing near the far end of the war ship as the crewmen began to lay the treasures before the angel Jaykal. The Bantu looked at the gold and sliver. They were afraid to touch the items.

"What are you doing?" the commander asked.

The Ram of God

"We are giving these things to the angel of God," many responded.

"No!" the commander yelled. The commander ran toward the treasure. Many of the Heruli took hold of him. The commander struggled as they tied his hands and his legs. They tied him to the mast.

The Bantu moved away from the treasure. They moved toward the angel Jaykal. The angel Jaykal did not move or speak.

The Heruli crewmen began to dance and shout. They yelled and screamed. The Bantu were afraid. The angel Jaykal did not move or speak.

"Help me! Help me!" the commander, yelled to the angel Jaykal. The angel Jaykal did not move or speak.

The Heruli crewmen yelled and screamed. Then, they stopped. Their swords were drawn and they held them to the commander.

"We freely give this treasure to your God!" one of the crewmen yelled, to the angel Jaykal.

The Heruli crewmen bowed toward the angel Jaykal.

"Take this treasure and leave us!" one of the crewmen yelled.

The angel Jaykal spoke, "God does not ask for gold, silver, and bronze."

The Heruli were startled. The angel Jaykal spoke.

The Ram of God

One of the Heruli crewmen stepped forward. He lowered his sword and he spoke, "What does your God ask?"

The angel Jaykal spoke. "God asks for what you can not give!"

The Heruli were puzzled. They looked at each other. "What does God ask that we can not give?" many asked.

"A sacrifice! God wants a sacrifice! We will kill the commander!" many yelled.

"No!" the commander yelled. "Help me!" he pleaded.

The angel Jaykal did not move or speak.

The Heruli crewmen began to dance and scream. They held their swords to the commander as to kill him. Then, they withdrew their swords. They yelled and screamed. Then, they stopped.

The Bantu were afraid. They moved closer towards the angel Jaykal.

The commander was bound to the mast of the war ship. He struggled to free himself as one of the crewmen approached him. The crewman's sword was held upward. He was to strike the commander. The commander bent his head downward. He prayed to God.

"Wait!" the commander ordered.

The crewman stopped.

The commander raised his head.

The Ram of God

"The God of the Christians has sent his angel to return these people from where they came. This God is a merciful God! The young girl said God will provide for us," the commander said.

"Provide what?" one of the crewmen asked.

"The young girl said God will give to us that which we need," the commander replied.

"What do we need?" one of the crewmen asked. "We have food. We have water."

"We needed food and water and God provided for us," the commander said. "The warship rested on the sand of an island we have not seen. On that island was food and fresh water."

The Heruli crewmen stopped. They looked at one another.

"The God of the Christians wants a sacrifice. When we have sacrificed you, he will leave!" one of the crewmen said.

"No!" the commander replied. "The angel Jaykal is to return these people from where they came. When this task is complete, he will leave."

"What of us? What will become of us?" many asked.

"I do not know," the commander replied.

"He will murder us!" one of the crewmen said.

"No!" the commander said. "The young girl said we are not to leave this ship. The young girl said we are not to harm these people. If we obey God's commands, the angel Jaykal will not harm us. The young girl said if you rebel, the angel of God will destroy all of you."

"He can not kill all of us!" one of the crewmen said.

The crewmen turned away from the commander. They looked at the angel Jaykal. The angel Jaykal stood near the drum. He did not move or speak.

The Bantu men, women, and children moved in front of the angel Jaykal. They were to protect him.

The Heruli crewmen held their swords. They began to slowly move towards the angel Jaykal. The Bantu men, women, and children moved backwards toward the angel Jaykal. They were to protect him.

The commander lowered his head. He prayed to God. He raised his head. "Stop! You can not defeat the angel of God! I will give you proof!" the commander yelled.

The Heruli crewmen stopped. They turned and looked at the commander.

"What proof?" many of the crewmen asked.

"The angel of God commands this warship. Look about! There are no sails! There is no wind! The warship moves at a speed greater than sail!" the commander yelled.

The Heruli crewmen looked about. They held their hands into the air. There was no wind. They looked to the mast. There was no sail. They looked to the sea. The sea was calm, yet the warship moved.

The Ram of God

The warship moved quickly through the calm waters.

"The angel of God is a servant of God! If the servant can do this thing, what can his master do?" the commander yelled.

The Heruli crewmen began to look at each other.

"The young girl healed all of the Bantu in the name of her God. Look at the Bantu men! Look at them!" the commander, yelled.

The Heruli crewmen looked at the Bantu men. The Bantu men stood in front of the angel Jaykal. They were to protect him.

"What are we to see?" one of the crewmen asked.

"Look at them! Look at their backs!" the commander, yelled.

One of the Heruli crewmen lowered his sword. He walked carefully toward one of the Bantu men. He carefully turned one of the Bantu men. The crewmen looked at his back.

"What are we to see?" many of the crewmen asked.

"There are no marks of the whip! The young girl healed the Bantu in the name of her God!" the commander yelled.

The crewmen gasped. It was true! There were no marks.

The crewman went to several of the Bantu men. He turned them towards the others. The crewmen gasped. There were no marks.

The Ram of God

"What God can heal the mark of the whip! What God can move a warship without wind or oar?" the commander yelled.

"This God sends his angel to return these people from where they came. The angel battles with a sword of fire! The fire consumes all it touches!" the commander yelled.

The Heruli crewmen looked at each other.

"This God provided food and water to us! This God will give to us that which we need," the commander yelled.

"We need nothing!" one of the crewmen said. "These things are tricks!"

The Heruli crewmen began to walk carefully towards the angel Jaykal. The Bantu men, women, and children moved backward towards the angel Jaykal. They were to protect him.

The commander lowered his head. He prayed to God. He quickly raised his head. "Stop!" he commanded.

The Heruli crewmen stopped. They turned and looked at the commander.

"I will give you proof!" the commander yelled.

"What proof?" one of the crewmen asked. "We need nothing!"

"Fish! Fish! We have no fish!" the commander yelled.

The Ram of God

The Heruli crewmen looked at each other. They did not have fish. The Bantu men, women, and children had eaten all of the fish.

"Where will we get fish?" one the crewmen asked. "Will they fall from the sky?"

The Heruli crewmen began to laugh.

"There are no fish in these waters. We are far from the land," one of the crewmen said.

"Cast the net into the sea! God will provide for us!" the commander yelled.

Several of the Heruli crewmen ran to the hold of the ship. They quickly returned with the fish net from the first hold and they cast the net into the sea.

The net jerked.

Several of the Heruli crewmen pulled the net. The net was filled with fish. There were many different kinds. They pulled the net onto the deck.

The Bantu began to yell. "Munga opoa maji!" - *God pulls fish from the water*.

The crewmen quickly placed the fish in straw baskets. They quickly cast the net into the sea.

The net did not jerk.

They pulled the net onto the deck. The net was empty.

"Where are the fish?" one of the crewmen asked.

The Ram of God

"God has given to us that which we needed. We needed fish and God provided for us. We do not need fish!" the commander yelled.

One Heruli crewman grunted. "There is no God!" he said.

"Yes! There is a God! The Christian God is a God of mercy who has sent his angel to return these people from where they came. You must ask forgiveness!" the commander yelled.

"Forgiveness of what?" one of the crewmen yelled.

"Forgiveness for what we have done to these people!" the commander yelled.

"These people are slaves! They are cattle to be bought and sold. I will not ask forgiveness for what I have done!" one of the crewmen yelled.

"It will take more than fish from the sea for me to ask forgiveness," the crewman added.

The Heruli crewmen turned towards the angel Jaykal. They began to slowly move towards him.

The commander lowered his head. He prayed to God. Quickly, he raised his head. "Stop!" he commanded.

The Heruli crewmen stopped. They turned to look at the commander.

"God gave to us that which we needed. We needed fish and God gave to us fish. We needed fresh water and God gave to us fresh water. Throw the fish into the sea! Throw the fresh water into the sea! God will give to us that which we need." The commander yelled.

The Heruli crewmen looked at one another. They quickly threw the fish net into the sea. They pulled the net from the sea. It was empty!

They threw the fish back into the sea. They cast the net. The net jerked. When they pulled the net onto the deck, it was full.

The Bantu saw these things. They turned towards the angel Jaykal and they bowed before him.

"What is this?" many of the crewmen said. They looked at the fish. There were many fish in the net.

"It is true! There is a God!" many of the crewmen said.

"Throw the water! Let us see for ourselves if this God will give to us that which we need," one of the crewmen yelled.

The Heruli crewman brought their casks of fresh water to the deck. They were to throw their fresh water into the sea. "No!" many of the crewmen yelled.

"No God can give us fresh water on the sea! We will die of thirst!" one of the crewmen yelled.

"If there is a God, he will provide water. If there is no God, we will die of thirst," one of the crewmen yelled.

"Only a God can turn saltwater into fresh water! Test God! We will see if God will provide for us," one of the crewmen yelled.

The Ram of God

"No!" many of the crewmen yelled. "There is no God! We will die of thirst!"

"I have seen many things of which I know not. The angel of God battles as no man of fact or myth. The warship moves without sail or oar. Many of my kinsmen died in white fire and I have seen an island where none existed. If there is a God, God will provide fresh water. Throw the water into the sea!" one of the crewmen yelled.

"No!" many of the crewmen yelled. "Do not throw all of our water into the sea."

The commander yelled, "Throw four casks into the sea! God will give to us that which we need! God will provide for us!"

The Heruli crewmen looked at each other. There were many casks of fresh water on the deck. The casks were open.

"We will test God!" one of the crewmen yelled. "Throw four casks into the sea. If God provides water, I will believe! I will ask forgiveness!"

The Heruli crewmen looked to each other. They nodded their heads. They will test God. If God provides water, they will believe. They will ask forgiveness.

Slowly, four of the crewmen each picked up a cask. They poured the fresh water into the sea. They placed the four empty casks onto the deck.

The Heruli crewmen looked at each other. Nothing happened.

They looked at the commander. Nothing happened.

The Ram of God

They looked at the Bantu. Nothing happened.

They looked at the angel Jaykal. Nothing happened.

Then, it began to rain.

The Heruli crewmen looked upwards. There were no clouds. The sky was clear. It was raining. The Bantu looked upwards. The rain fell very softly. Then, it began to rain very quickly.

The Bantu began to yell. "Munga mvua bila kikomo!" - *God brings the rain*.

They looked at the empty water casks. The casks began to fill very quickly. When the casks were full, the rain stopped.

The Heruli crewmen looked to the angel Jaykal. He stood beside the drum. He did not move or speak. They looked at his clothes. The rain did not fall onto him. He was not wet. They looked to each other. Their clothes were dry. They were not wet. The rain did not fall onto them. They looked to the four water casks. The casks were filled with fresh rainwater.

"Praise God!" the commander yelled.

Many of the Heruli crewmen walked to the four casks of water. They slowly dipped their hands into the water and they tasted it.

"It is fresh water!" one of the crewmen said. He turned to the others. "Rain fell from a empty sky."

The Heruli crewmen gathered around the four casks and they tasted the fresh water. "There is a

God! God provided for us!" many of the crewmen said.

"The Christians are correct! There is a God!" one of the crewmen said.

"The stories are true!" he added.

"What stories?" one crewman, asked.

"The Christians worship the Son of God. His name is Jesus," the crewman replied.

One of the Heruli crewmen pushed his way toward the four water casks. "I know of Jesus! He is the Son of God! He died and God rose him from the dead," the crewman said.

The Heruli crewmen looked toward the angel Jaykal. One of them pointed toward the angel Jaykal. "Is that Jesus?" he asked.

"No!" one of the crewmen replied. "Jesus is in heaven with God. That is one of God's angels."

"This is a good and kind God! He sent his warrior to return these people from where we took them," one of the crewmen said.

"Yes! God is good and kind! God protects the weak and the defenseless," one of the crewmen said.

"We defied God's command! The young girl said God commanded us to return the Bantu and we refused," one of the crewmen said.

"We were foolish to defy God! God protects these people! God is kind and just!" one of the crewmen said.

The Ram of God

The Heruli crewmen released their swords. They kneeled on the deck before the angel Jaykal. They clasped their hands and they began to pray.

"Forgive us!" many, said.

"There is a God! God protects these people! God provided for us!" one of the crewmen said.

"We ask God's forgiveness for what we have done," one of the crewmen said.

The angel Jaykal stood before the large drum. He looked at the Heruli crewmen knelled before him. He heard them pray to God for forgiveness.

"God knows what is in every man's heart. I will return these people from where they came. You will take no other," the angel Jaykal said.

The Heruli crewmen looked upward at the angel Jaykal.

"You have given to God what God asks. God forgives you," the angel Jaykal said.

The Heruli and the Bantu began to shout and cheer. "Praise God!" the Heruli crewmen yelled. The commander was quickly untied.

The Bantu yelled. "Munga kaga!" - *God protects us*.

Day Four - The Feast to God

The Heruli and the Bantu shared the food and fresh water. They danced and laughed. Many times they fell to their knees before the angel Jaykal. They prayed to God. They asked God for his blessing.

The angel Jaykal did not move or speak.

The warship moved quickly through the calm waters. The sun was near its height when they saw the land. The warship had brought them to where they had come. The warship rested gently on a sand bar. The Heruli helped the Bantu men, women, and children to leave the ship.

The angel Jaykal stood by the drum. He did not move or speak.

The Heruli crewmen removed the food from the warship. Together, the Heruli and the Bantu held a feast. They held a feast to God. They danced and they laughed. Many times they stopped to pray. They gave thanks to God.

The next morning, the Heruli were to leave. The Bantu brought them fruit, fish, and fresh water. The warship was quickly loaded and the Heruli climbed aboard their ship.

The angel Jaykal stood by the drum. He did not move or speak.

The commander walked carefully towards the drum. As he neared the drum, the warship moved gently away from the sand bar. The warship turned toward open sea.

The Ram of God

"What is this?" the commander asked the angel Jaykal. "The Bantu have been returned from where they came. We asked God to forgive us."

"What does God ask of us?" he added.

The angel Jaykal spoke. "Look into your heart. God will guide you." The angel Jaykal became as a shadow before him.

The commander and the Heruli crewmen looked at each other. They looked to the sky. There was no wind, yet the warship moved. They looked to the shore and there were many Bantu looking towards them. The warship moved slowly toward open sea.

"Raise the sail!" the commander ordered.

The crew ran quickly to raise the sail. As the large sail was unfurled, the image of the ram was exposed. Then, wind filled the sail.

The Heruli warship moved quickly toward the open sea.

The Bantu stayed where the warship had left them. They built huts and they began to live near the sea. A village grew where none had been. God gave to them all they needed. There were fish, fruits, and fresh water.

Word quickly spread of the child healer. Many people came to see Habib. The Bantu said God blesses Habib. God heals through the hands of Habib. All who are sick are healed when Habib touches them. The Bantu came and looked at the child.

The child was like any other.

The Bantu did not believe the child was a poza. The Bantu heard many stories of the young girl that healed the ill Bantu on the slave ship. They heard the story of God's angel defeating the Heruli with a sword of fire. They heard of God blessing Habib. They saw nothing. The child did nothing. The child was one year of age.

Many Bantu came to the village of the rescued Bantu. They stood and they waited. They waited for something to happen.

God Heals the Bantu Child

The Bantu man ran quickly through the jungle. In his arms he carried his daughter. She was but five years in age. Far behind him, his wife and many of his kinsmen followed. Farther behind, the man healer followed.

The Bantu man was very tired but he ran. His daughter was limp in his arms. He looked at her as he ran and tears streamed down his cheeks. He ran as fast as he could. He ran to the village of the rescued Bantu. He ran to the Mwana Poza.

The Bantu man neared the village and he began to yell, "Nyoka kumbwe!" - *Snake bite*.

Many of the Bantu heard his cry and they ran towards his voice. "Nyoka kumbwe!" the man yelled. In his arms was the almost lifeless body of his daughter. A snake had struck his daughter on her leg. The man healer attempted to remove the poison but he could not. The man healer worked his magic but the magic did not cure the young girl. The young girl's leg began to swell where the snake struck her and the young girl fell limp and she closed her eyes. The man healer said no one could help her.

The young girl's father heard stories of a Mwana Poza. He picked up his daughter and he began to run towards the village of the rescued Bantu. His wife and many others followed.

The man healer was angered. His magic was great. No one possessed his magic. The child would die. The man healer ran after them.

The Bantu man ran towards the village. He yelled, "Nyoka kumbwe!" As he neared the village, many Bantu men met him. He was very tired. One man took his daughter from him and he ran towards the hut of Habib. He yelled, "Nyoka kumbwe!"

The Bantu had heard the man's cry and they quickly gathered at Habib's hut. They waited to see what would happen.

The child was brought quickly before Habib's hut. The man carefully placed the child on the grass before the hut. Her leg was swollen where the snake struck her. The young girl lay almost lifeless before the hut of Habib.

The young girl's father ran to her and he lay beside her. His wife and the kinsmen of his village quickly ran to her. They lay beside her. The man healer quickly approached and he stood near. He watched them.

Many Bantu stood before the hut of Habid. They waited for something to happen. They looked to the opening of Habib's hut. They saw no one. No one exited the hut.

The Ram of God

They looked at the young girl who lay before the hut. She was near death. Beside her, her mother and father lay on the ground. They bowed toward the hut of Habib.

They prayed, "Munga Poza." - *God Heal.*

The young girl's kinsmen lay on the ground. They bowed toward the hut of Habib.

They prayed, "Munga Poza."

Many of the Bantu began to chant, " Munga Poza."

The man healer stood near them. He was angered. His magic was great. No one possessed his magic. The child would die. No one could save her.

Habib slowly exited the hut. He was but one year in age. Habib looked at the young girl then he looked at the chanting Bantu.

"Munga Poza," the Bantu chanted.

Habib looked upward. He began to walk slowly toward the young girl. He came close to her and he kneeled before her.

The Bantu stopped chanting. They all kneeled before Habib.

The man healer did not kneel. He stood looking at Habib.

Habib looked at the young girl then he looked at the kneeling Bantu.

The Bantu began to chant, "Munga Poza!"

Habib looked upward then he reached his hand out toward the young girl. He touched her leg. He touched the leg that was swollen.

The Bantu gasped.

The man healer gasped.

The leg became as the other leg. The young girl opened her eyes and she stood.

God Destroys the Man Healer in Fire

The Bantu looked at the young girl. God healed through the hands of Habib. Habib was a Mwana Poza.

The man healer was angered. His magic had been defeated. In his hands, he held his knife. He ran towards Habib and he yelled, "Ogopa mwana!" - *Be afraid of the child*.

The Bantu were knelled before Habib. They turned to see the man healer running towards Habib. In his hands, he held a knife.

The man healer yelled, "Ogopa mwana!" He quickly neared Habib.

The man healer ran to Habib and he stood before him. Habib sat on the grass looking upward. The young girl healed by God stood beside him.

The Bantu were startled. They looked at Habib and the man healer.

The man healer raised his knife to strike Habib.

"Kifo!" - *Death*. The man healer yelled.

The Ram of God

Suddenly, the knife in the man healer's hand became as of fire. The fire quickly covered the body of the man healer. Then, the fire was gone. The man healer was gone. The fire of God consumed him.

The Bantu slowly rose to their feet. They did not know what they had seen. God healed the young girl through the hand's of Habib. Then, God destroyed the man healer in fire.

God gave life to the young girl and God gave death to the man healer.

"Munga fisha mganguzi," - *God put to death witch doctor*. One of the Bantu men said.

"Munga kaga mwana poza," - *God protects the child healer*. One of the Bantu men said.

"Munga poza Bantu mwana," - *God healed Bantu child*. Many of the Bantu women said.

The Bantu kneeled. "Himidi Munga," - *Praise God*. They chanted.

The young girl's mother and father slowly stood and they walked to her. They held to her and they bowed to Habib.

"Himidi Munga," they said.

Habib slowly stood. He turned and walked toward his hut. His mother stood waiting for him. Habib walked past her into the hut.

The Bantu began to shout and cheer.

God Heals the Bantu Village

Many weeks passed and the Bantu celebrated the Mwana Poza. Word of the child healer quickly spread among the Bantu villages. One morning, many Bantu men came to the village of the rescued Bantu. They came from a village far away.

The Bantu men came before the hut of Habib. Habib's mother walked out of her hut to greet them. The Bantu men kneeled.

"Munga kaga Bantu," - *God protects Bantu*. One of the Bantu men said.

"Munga kaga mwana poza," - *God protects child healer*. One of the Bantu men said.

The men pointed to the village. Then they pointed to themselves and they pointed far from the village.

"Kijiji maradhi," - *Village has sickness*. The Bantu men said.

The Bantu men pointed away from the village. They pointed far away.

"Munga poza kijiji," - *God heal village*. The men said.

The Bantu men wanted Habib to come with them. They wanted Habib to come to their village. There was much illness in their village.

Habib's mother nodded her head. They would come with them.

The Ram of God

Word quickly spread through the village that the Mwana Poza was going to others and many of the Bantu assembled. They would go with Habib. They wanted to witness God heal others.

The Bantu assembled and one of the Bantu men held to Habib. They began to walk toward the other village. One of the men from the other village walked first. He held to Habib. Habib's mother followed him. Then, the entire Bantu village followed. Men, women, and children followed. They followed Habib.

The Bantu walked for three days. They stopped many times to eat and rest. They did not stop to sleep. It was near sunset when they arrived at the Bantu village.

The village was quite. They saw no one walking about. There was no one to greet them and no fires burned before the huts. The Bantu stopped near the village and one of the men carried Habib forward. Habib's mother followed.

There were many huts and they appeared to be empty. The Bantu kneeled near the edge of the village and they began to chant. "Mungubariki Bantu!" - *God bless Bantu.*

The man carried Habib into a hut and Habib's mother followed.

The Bantu waited. Then, the man carrying Habib walked out of the hut. Habib's mother followed and they walked into another hut.

A man, women, and three children exited the first hut. They kneeled to the ground and they yelled, "Munga poza Bantu," - *God heals Bantu.*

"Munga poza maradhi," - *God heals sickness*. They yelled.

The man carrying Habib entered and exited many huts. When he exited, men, women, and children exited after him. God healed the Bantu. God healed through the hands of Habib.

Habib was carried to every hut. God healed all of the Bantu.

The Bantu began to shout and yell. Then, they became very quite. They all kneeled. Men, women, and children kneeled. They spoke softly, "Himidi Munga," - *Praise God.*

The Ram of God

The Heruli had been gone for many months. The Bantu village, where the rescued Bantu were left, had expanded. Many Bantu came to the village to see the Mwana Poza. When they came, they stayed. The Bantu wanted to be near Habib. They wanted to be near God.

They witnessed many Bantu healed by God. One child was born blind. God healed the child through the hands of Habib. A young boy injured his leg. His leg was dark black where he cut it and the young boy was ill with fever. God healed the young boy's leg when Habib touched it. God healed all that Habib touched.

One morning, the Bantu saw a ship nearing their village. They looked to the ship and there was a large sail. On the sail was the head of an animal. The animal was a ram. The Heruli had returned!

The Ram of God

"Beberu mtumwa jahazi!" - *The ram slave ship.* The Bantu yelled.

The Bantu were frightened. The Heruli had captured them and now they had returned. The Heruli were to take others. The Bantu ran. They hid in the jungle.

The warship slowly neared the land and stopped in shallow water. The Bantu watched from the jungle. From where they were hidden, they could see many on the deck of the ship. Then, Bantu men, women, and children began to leave the ship. There were many of their kinsmen.

The Heruli helped the Bantu to the sand. There were many that were ill and hungry. There were many Heruli who were injured.

The Bantu watched from where they were hidden in the jungle. They watched the Heruli help the Bantu to the beach.

One Bantu man leapt from the side of the ship into the water. He began to run through the surf to the sand.

"Jaha! Habib!" he yelled. The Bantu man was Tomi, Habib's father.

Habib's mother heard his cries and she ran from the jungle. She held to Habib and she ran to her husband. "Tomi!" she yelled.

Slowly, the Bantu left from where they hid. They walked slowly toward the sand.

The Ram of God

The freed Bantu cried out. They had been taken as slaves. The Heruli rescued them. The Heruli battled others to guard and protect them.

"Munga kaga!" - *God protects us*. The freed Bantu yelled.

The freed Bantu yelled to their kinsmen. They pointed to the Heruli warship. They pointed to the sail with the image of the ram.

"Beberu Munga kaga!" - *The Ram of God protects us*. The freed Bantu yelled

The Bantu came from hiding. They ran quickly to the sand to help their kinsmen and the Heruli.

Jaha, Tomi, and Habib stood on the sand. They watched as the Bantu took many of the Heruli and their kinsmen from the ship.

There were many Heruli injured and there were many ill Bantu. The Bantu lay them on the sand.

Then, the Bantu turned and looked toward Habib.

Jaha stood Habib on the sand. Habib looked upward and he began to walk to the injured Heruli and the ill Bantu. He touched them. He touched them all. When Habib touched them, God healed them.

The Bantu did not know what they had seen. Their enemy was their protector. God healed the injured Heruli and the ill Bantu. God healed all that Habib touched.

The Bantu began to shout and cheer.

The Ram of God

The Heruli stayed at the village for many days. Then, they were to leave. The Bantu placed food and fresh water on the ship. The Heruli boarded their ship and the ship headed towards open sea.

God's Warriors

The slave ship moved on the open sea. The wind was strong and the sail was full. The crew laughed and drank wine. Below the upper deck, many Bantu men, women, and children huddled together. They were afraid.

The Bantu men were chained together. On their backs were the marks of a whip. The women cried from fear and the children cried from hunger.

The Bantu were afraid to speak. Many of the crew of the slave ship walked among them. They held whips to beat them and the crew ate food in front of them. The Bantu were hungry and thirsty.

On the deck of the slave ship, one of the crew looked outward toward open sea.

"Look!" the crewman, yelled.

Many of the crew ran towards the bow of their ship. Far away was another ship.

"Who is it?" the commander asked.

The crew of the slave ship looked toward the open sea. The ship was quickly approaching them. They looked to the sail. On the sail was the image of an animal. The image was a great ram.

The Ram of God

"Turn!" the commander, yelled. One of the crewmen moved the rudder and the ship quickly turned.

The ship with the ram's sail turned in the same direction.

"It's coming fast!" one of the crewmen yelled.

The commander ran to the door that led to the hold of the ship. He quickly opened it and he yelled to the crew below. "Quickly! We are to be boarded! One-half stay below!"

Many of the crew in the hold quickly came up the ladder.

The crew stood on the deck. They watched the ship following them.

The ship with the ram's head on its sail quickly overtook the slave ship. As it neared, the crew of the slave ship saw many warriors on the deck. The warriors held swords and shields.

"They're going to ram us!" one of the crewmen yelled.

The crew of the slave ship braced themselves. The ship with the ram's head on its sail rammed them.

Braaak!

The bow of the ship with the ram's head struck the front of the slave ship and the slave ship jerked. The crew of the slave ship was thrown to the deck.

Rrruuuuuk!

The Ram of God

The ship with the ram on its sail was aside the slave ship. Immediately, many ropes were thrown to hold the ships together. Then, the warriors boarded the slave ship.

The warriors were fierce. The warriors fought the crew of the slave ship. They pushed them backward with their shields and swords.

The warriors quickly fought their way to the hold of the ship. The hold was thrown open and many of the warriors entered the first hold. The warriors fought their way to the Bantu.

One of the warriors yelled out to the Bantu. "Heruli mlinzi wa Bantu," - *Heruli protector of the Bantu.*

The Bantu were startled to hear their language.

The warriors fought the crew of the slave ship in the hold. The warriors pushed the crew backward. Then, the warriors quickly unchained the Bantu men.

"Fuata!" - *Follow.* The Heruli warriors yelled.

The Bantu men, women, and children were amazed. The warriors spoke their language. Quickly, they followed the fierce Heruli up the ladder. The fierce warriors pushed the crew of the slave ship backward with their shields and swords. The Bantu followed the Heruli to the ship with the great ram on its sail.

The Bantu were afraid. All around them the fierce Heruli battled the crew of the slave ship. The warriors pushed the crew of the slave ship backward with their shields and swords. They pushed them away from the fleeing Bantu.

The Ram of God

"Fuata!" The Heruli warriors yelled.

The Bantu men, women, and children followed the warriors to the Heruli ship. When the Bantu were safely aboard the Heruli warship the commander yelled to his men, "Quickly! Leave them to God's justice!"

As quickly as the ship with the ram's head on its sail came, it left.

The crew of the slave ship was shaken. Many of the crew was injured in battle. The Heruli were fierce. They battled to rescue the captured Bantu.

The commander looked toward the open sea. The ship with the ram's head was far ahead of them. He looked to his men. His men were defeated. Many had been struck on their arms and legs. There was no dead.

One of the crewmen ran to the commander. "The gold! The gold is safe! They did not take the gold!" the crewman said.

"The slaves! They took the slaves!" one of the crewmen yelled.

One of the crewmen walked toward the commander. On his face were many bruises. He held to his arm. A sword had struck his arm. "We will take others," he said.

"No!" the commander yelled.

The commander turned to his men. "We were defeated! They could have killed all of us but they did not! They did not want our gold. They only wanted to rescue the slaves," the commander said.

"One of the warriors yelled that God will seek his justice upon us. If we take others, they will return. If they return, they will kill all of us."

"They did not kill us! We will take others! We will be prepared for them," one of the crewmen said.

"No!" the commander yelled.

"They are God's justice! If we battle, they will kill us! We can not defeat God! We can not defeat God's warriors! God has warned us! We will take no others!" the commander yelled.

"I know of that ship!" one of the crew yelled. "The ram on the sail! The ship sails to free God's people! The ship is the Ram of God!"

The crew of the slave ship began to look to each other. "The Ram of God!" they said.

"God has warned us not to take others. If we take others, the Ram of God will destroy us!" the crewman added.

The crewmen of the slave ship lowered their heads. They looked far out to the sea. The ship with the ram's sail slowly disappeared over the horizon. The crew turned and they began to care for the wounded.

The Beberu Munga

Many months passed and one morning, the Bantu saw the ship. A ship was heading toward the land. They looked to the ships sail. On the sail was the image of an animal. The image was a ram. The ship was the Heruli. The Heruli had returned.

The Ram of God

"Beberu Munga!" - *The Ram of God*. The Bantu yelled.

"Beberu Munga uchaji mtumwa mashua!" - *The Ram of God brings fear to the slave ships*. The Bantu yelled.

"Munga kaga mtwana mjakazi mwana mtumwa!" - *God protects men, women, children slaves*. The Bantu yelled.

The Bantu ran to the sand to greet them. The ship slowly neared the land and stopped in shallow water. The Bantu swam to the ship. On board the ship were many Bantu men, women, and children. The Heruli had rescued them. The Heruli had returned them home.

The Heruli had received many injuries. There were many that could not leave the ship. They could not come to Habib, Habib was taken to them. The first level of the war ship held many that were injured. Habib touched them and God healed them. Habib was taken to the second level. There were two Heruli who were dead. They had been killed in battle. Habib did not touch them. The dead Heruli were taken to the land where they were buried.

That night there was a great feast. The rescued Bantu told stories of the Heruli who boarded the ship and battled to save them. The Bantu spoke of the sail and of the image of the animal. They spoke of the head of a ram. They spoke of the Ram of God.

They spoke of the Beberu Munga.

The Bantu were taken from many ships. The Heruli boarded the ship and battled with the crew to free them. They were taken to the Ram of God where they were given food and water. The Heruli cared for them.

The Bantu spoke that the men on the ship were afraid when they saw the sail with the animal head. They were afraid of the Ram of God. The men knew God commanded the ship. The men knew God had sent the ship to return the Bantu men, women, and children from where they came.

The Bantu laughed and danced. Then, they became very quiet. They walked to where the Heruli were buried. They kneeled before the two graves.

The Bantu were very quiet. The Heruli had rescued them and two Heruli were killed. They died saving others.

"Munga bariki Heruli mpiganaji," - *God bless Heruli warriors*. They chanted.

The Bantu men, women, and children wept. They wept for the fallen warriors.

The Bantu slowly stood and they returned to their huts.

The Heruli stayed at the village for several days. Then, they were to leave. The Bantu placed food and fresh water on the warship. The Heruli were to board their ship when they saw two young Bantu men standing near the warship. The Bantu men were clothed in war clothing. They wore the skin of a lion and they held war spears. On the end of their spears was the carving of an animal. The carving was the head of a ram.

The Ram of God

The Heruli held up their swords. They thought the Bantu men were to attack them. The two Bantu men lowered their spears.

"Munga vita mtumwa mashua!" - *God wars on the slave ship*. They said.

"Munga kaga mwana poza!" - *God protects the child healer*. They said.

"Heruli kaga mjakazi mtwana mwana mtumwa!" - *Heruli protects man, woman, child slave*. They said.

"Mtumwa mashua uchaji afrino!" - *Slave ships are afraid of the ram*. They said.

The two Bantu men pointed to the end of their war spears. On the end of the war spear was the carving of a ram's head.

"Bantu pigana afrino mkuki kaga Bantu mtumwa!" - *Bantu fights with ram spear to protect Bantu slave*. They said.

"Bantu pigana. Fuma beberu!" - *Bantu fight. Strike with spear with ram*. They said.

The Heruli crewmen did not understand what the two Bantu men said.

The two Bantu men motioned for the Heruli to follow them. The two Bantu men walked to where the two Herlui were buried. They motioned to the two graves and they motioned to themselves. The two Bantu men pointed at the warship.

"Munga vita mtumwa jahazi!" - *God wars on the slave ship*. They said.

The Ram of God

"Bantu vita mtumwa jahazi!" - *Bantu wars on the slave ship*. They said.

The two Bantu men pointed to the Heruli crewmen and they pointed towards the graves of the two dead Heruli. The two Bantu men pointed to themselves.

"Bantu Heruli pigana mtumwa jahazi Beberu Munga!" - *Bantu and Heruli fight slave ship with Ram of God.* They said.

The two Bantu men were to replace the two Heruli that died saving their kinsmen.

The Heruli kneeled on the grass. The two Bantu men kneeled on the grass.

"We give to God what God asks!" the commander said.

The Heruli rose. The two Bantu men rose. The commander pointed toward the warship. "Come with us! Come with us to do God's will!" the commander said.

The Bantu men jumped and yelled. The Bantu began to scream and shout. The Bantu men were to join the Ram of God.

The Bantu ran to the beach. They yelled and screamed as the two Bantu men climbed aboard the Ram of God. The two Bantu warriors stood on the deck of the Heruli warship. They raised their spears and they pointed to the great ram on the sail. The Bantu on the beach yelled and screamed.

Then, they all kneeled. They prayed to God to guard and protect them. They prayed to God to guard and protect captured Bantu slaves.

The warship slowly turned toward open sea. The Bantu watched the warship slowly sail out of their sight.

God Heals the Lions

The Bantu waited for the Beberu Munga to return. One morning, Habib exited his hut. Habib was six years in age. He stood before his hut and he looked to the east.

Jaha and Tomi exited the hut. They looked at Habib. Habib just stood. He did not speak. Habib looked toward the east.

"Habib," Tomi called.

Habib did not speak or answer. He stood looking toward the east.

Many of the Bantu came to Habib's hut. They looked at him. Habib stood looking toward the east.

"Cimba tak!" - *Lion cry for help*. Habib said.

The Bantu were startled! The lions were in the grassland. They were far from the village. They heard no sound. They heard no cry.

"Cimba tak!" Habib yelled. Then, he began to run. He ran towards the east. Habib ran towards the grassland.

Many of the Bantu men ran to their huts. They quickly picked up their spears and their shields. They ran after Habib. They ran toward the grassland.

The Ram of God

Habib ran very fast. They had traveled far when the Bantu men stopped. They heard it! They heard the cry of the lion.

"Cimba gong," - *Lion cry in pain*. Many of the Bantu men yelled. The Bantu men followed Habib. They ran to the edge of the jungle. They ran to the grassland and they stopped.

There before them were many lions. The lions were lying on their sides and crying in pain. There were males and females. There were many cubs.

Two female lions walked quickly before the lions. The females cried in pain. They walked and stumbled. Then, they slowly stood. The two females guarded the fallen lions.

The Bantu men looked near the jungle. There was a small pond of water. Near the water were several antelope. The antelope were dead. They had been partially eaten. They looked to the water. The water was dark black.

Near the two female lions, Habib stood. He stood near the lions. The Bantu men raised their spears.

"Jimad!" - *Stop*. Habib yelled.

The Bantu men lowered their spears. They watched the two female lions walk before the others. The two female lions stumbled and fell. They did not get up. The lions cried in pain.

"Cimba nyo dung jiji!" - *Lion drink poison from waterhole*. One of the Bantu men yelled.

"Cimba kem Munga!" - *Lion cry out for God*. One of the Bantu men yelled.

"Munga jatab!" - *God answer call*. One of the Bantu men yelled.

"Bantu jatab!" - *Bantu answer call*. One of the Bantu men yelled.

One of the Bantu men ran before the others. He pointed toward the dead antelope near the poisoned water. "Cab bUgUm babada!" - *Act quickly burn antelope*. He yelled.

The Bantu men ran quickly to the edge of the water. They held to the legs of the dead antelope and they pulled them from the water. They quickly pulled them to the jungle.

The Bantu men gathered dried branches and they started a fire. Then, the dead antelope were thrown onto the fire.

Habib stood in the short grass. The rains had begun and the water had filled the small pond. Something in the pond poisoned the water. The thirsty antelope had drunk from the pond. They died. The lions had eaten of the antelope and drank of the water.

The lions were dying. They cried out in pain.

Habib walked slowly toward the lions. One of the female lions stood. She was shaking and she roared at Habib. Habib stopped and he held his hand up.

"CIetUk!" - *Move*. Habib commanded.

The female lion shook. She began to walk and she fell. The female lion cried in pain.

The Ram of God

Habib walked to the fallen lion and he kneeled. The female lion cried in pain. Habib reached out to her. He touched her.

"DibUp!" - *Be strong, be healthy*. He said.

The female lion stood. She stood and she moved away from Habib.

"Munga poza cimba," - *God heal lion*. Many of the Bantu men said.

The Bantu men watched Habib move from lion to lion. He kneeled before them and he touched them.

"DibUp!" - *Be strong, be healthy*. He said.

The lions stood. God healed the lions. The lions stood and they moved away from Habib. The lions moved far from Habib. They did not attack him. The lions watched Habib move from lion to lion. Then, Habib walked toward the poisoned pond.

Habib walked to the pond and he stood before the edge. Then, he looked upward. Habib whispered and he entered the water. He began to walk in the water.

The Bantu men gasped. As Habib walked in the water, the color changed. The black became clear. Habib walked out of the water.

Habib looked at the Bantu men. He pointed towards the lions. "Munga poza cimba. Munga poza jiji," - *God heal lion. God heals waterhole*. He said.

The Bantu men watched Habib walk towards them. When Habib came to the edge of the jungle, the lions ran towards the water. They quickly lapped the water. Then, many antelope came to the water.

The Ram of God

The lions did not attack the antelope. The antelope and the lion drank from the small waterhole.

The Bantu men did not know what they had seen. God healed the lions and God healed the water. Then, the lion and the antelope drank from the pond.

Several of the Bantu men ran to the village. They gathered the Bantu and they all came to the edge of the jungle. They came to the grassland.

The Bantu stood at the edge of the jungle and they watched the lions and the antelope drink from the water. They had not seen such a thing.

Then, they all kneeled. They spoke softly, "Himidi Munga," - *Praise God.*

The Water of Peace

Many days passed and one morning Habib went to each hut. Habib went to the hut and he yelled, "Fuata," - *Follow.*

The Bantu quickly assembled. When they were assembled, Habib pointed towards the east. "Fuata!" he said.

Habib began to walk towards the east. He walked towards the grassland. The Bantu followed. They all followed Habib.

The Bantu came to the grassland and they stopped at the edge of the jungle. There before them were many animals. There were lions, antelope, monkeys, and birds. The small waterhole was very large. The grass was tall and green.

The Ram of God

The animals drank from the clear water of the waterhole. The lions and the antelope drank together. The lions did not attack the antelope. The birds and the monkeys drank from the cool water.

The Bantu had not seen such a thing. The animals were at peace. They drank from the cool water without fear.

Habib pointed toward the waterhole. "Diba banga Tende," - *Water of Peace*. He said.

"Nyo," - *Drink*. He added.

The Bantu looked at the water and they looked at Habib. Then, they looked at all of the animals that were drinking the water. The animals were at peace with one another. They did not drink in fear.

One Bantu woman stepped from the others. She walked from the edge of the jungle towards the waterhole. The animals looked upwards toward her.

She did not stop. She was not afraid.

The lions looked at her. They did not roar at her or charge her. The lions lay in the tall, cool grass.

The woman walked to the waterhole. Beside her, a male lion was lapping the water. The lion looked upwards at her.

"Himidi Munga," - *Praise God.* The woman said.

The lion lowered his head and he lapped the cool water. The Bantu woman kneeled and she dipped her hand into the water. She drank from the Water of Peace.

The Ram of God

The Bantu began to walk to the waterhole. The lions did not roar at them or charge them. The Bantu came to the waterhole. They kneeled and drank of the Water of Peace.

Habib stood near the jungle. He watched as the Bantu and the animals drank together. He looked upward and he smiled.

The Bantu stood and they held hands. They looked all around them. There were many animals. The animals drank from the cool water. The animals were at peace with one another.

The Bantu stood among the lions and the lions did not roar at them or charge them. They stood together.

The Bantu understood what they had seen.

They were one of God's creations. They, like the animals, were of God. They were at peace with one another. The Bantu prayed to God to help them. The Bantu prayed to God to free them. God heard their prayers.

God forgave the Heruli and the Bantu forgave the Heruli. They were as one. They looked at each other and they smiled. There was no hate or anger among them. They loved one another. They loved each other as brother and sister.

They were one. The Bantu were one with God.

The Bantu looked upward. They held their hands upward.

"Himidi Munga," - *Praise God.* They said.

One Year Later

The Heruli warship returned many times. At first, there were many Heruli injured in battle. Then, the Heruli returned with no injuries. Many spoke of the Ram of God sent by God to return captured Bantu to their home. The slave ships were afraid when they saw the sail with the ram's head. The crewmen of the slave ship did not battle. They freely returned the captured Bantu.

Many times the Heruli warship returned with no rescued Bantu. Slowly, the slave ships stopped coming. They stopped coming because they were afraid of the Ram of God. One day, the Heruli warship returned. There were no captured Bantu.

Habib was seven years of age. He was waiting on the beach for the Heruli warship. Behind Habib, the Bantu waited. The Bantu village was once small, now it was large. There were many Bantu. When the warship stopped in shallow water, Habib walked from the sand to the water. He walked alone. He entered the water and he swam to the ship.

Habib swam to the ship and he climbed aboard. The commander was waiting for him. The two Bantu warriors had taught the commander their language.

Habib spoke to the commander. "God has spoken to me in prayer. You have given to God what God asked. You will return to your country."

"Who will protect the Bantu?" the commander asked.

"God will send others," Habib replied.

The Ram of God

The commander and the Heruli crewmen bowed. "We obey God's command," the commander said.

The commander raised his head. "What does God ask of you?" the commander asked.

"God sends me to another," Habib replied. He pointed toward the jungle. "I am to travel far away."

The commander and the Heruli crewmen bowed to Habib.

The commander raised his head. "I give this to God! I give this to you," the commander said. The commander reached to his neck. On his neck was a necklace. He removed the necklace and he handed it to Habib.

The chain of the necklace was made of bronze. Attached to the bronze chain was a small bronze circle. On the bronze circle was the symbol of the Heruli, a ram.

"This ram is a symbol of God's power. This ram is a symbol of God's love," the commander said.

Habib took the necklace and he pulled it over his head.

The commander and the Heruli crewmen bowed to Habib.

Habib and the two Bantu warriors left the warship and the ship was quickly loaded with food and fresh water.

The Bantu stood on the sand as the warship slowly turned toward open sea. The large sail glistened in the sun. The Bantu could see the sail. They saw the image of the ram.

The Bantu kneeled on the sand. They bowed toward the great ram. "Himidi Munga!" - *Praise God*. The Bantu chanted.

God's warriors had completed their task. They had rescued and freed many Bantu slaves. The Beberu Munga protected the Bantu. Now, the Beberu Munga headed homeward.

The Bantu kneeled on the sand. They watched the Beberu Munga slowly sail out of their sight. When the Beberu Munga was gone, they rose to their feet.

Habib turned and he walked away from the beach. His mother and his father were waiting for him. Habib was to travel far away. He was to travel to many villages far in the jungle.

Habib would share God's blessing with others.

The Bantu waited for Habib. There were many Bantu. Word quickly spread that the Mwana Poza was to leave the village. God sends the Mwana Poza to others. The Bantu left their villages. They left everything and they traveled to the village of the Mwana Poza.

Habib began to walk towards the jungle. His mother and his father walked beside him. Behind Habib, there were many Bantu. Men, women, and children followed.

One Month Later

The sun had long disappeared and there were many fires in the jungle. Habib stood before a large fire. Bantu men, women, and children gathered near.

Habib had traveled to many villages. As he neared a village, runners ran before him. The runners ran to the village and they told of the Mwana Poza. The Bantu gathered their ill and they placed them at the edge of their village. Habib entered the village and he touched them. God healed all he touched. The blind began to see and the cripples walked. The ill and the infirmed were made whole.

Habib spoke to the Bantu. He told them of God. He told them of God's blessing. Then, he left the village. He left the village to travel to another. He traveled to share the blessing of God.

Many Bantu followed Habib. It was night and they had stopped to eat, rest, and sleep. Tomorrow, Habib would travel to another village. Tomorrow, Habib would share the blessing of God with others.

They traveled south. They were far from the sea.

Habib stood before the large fire and he began to speak.

"Himidi Munga!" - *Praise God.*

"Bwana Asifiwe!" - *Praise the Lord.*

The Bantu lowered their heads and they repeated Habib's last words. "Bwana Asifiwe," - *Praise the Lord.*

The Ram of God

Habib began to walk around the large fire. He looked upward to the night sky. The stars were bright. He held his hands upward toward the stars and he smiled.

He lowered his hands and he looked at the Bantu who sat before him. There were many hundreds of men, women, and children.

The Bantu villages were abandoned.

Habib entered a village and God healed all he touched. Habib told them of God and God's blessing. When Habib left the village, the Bantu followed. The Bantu abandoned their village and they followed him.

They followed him to hear his words.

They followed him to learn of God's blessing.

The Bantu raised their heads and Habib began to speak.

"Bin Munga Bwana Yesu," - *Lord Jesus is the Son of God.*

"Ondoka kwa dhamba watu wote Bwana Yesu," - *Lord Jesus died for the sin of all people.*

The Bantu lowered their heads. They spoke softly. "Bwana Yesu Asifiwe," - *Praise Lord Jesus.*

They raised their heads and Habib began to speak.

"Kipofu kubwa tumai Bwana Yesu," - *The blind man had great faith in Lord Jesus.*

The Ram of God

The Bantu legend of the "Beberu Munga"

In the year 600 AD, missionaries traveled to Africa to teach Christianity to the Bantu. The Bantu lived near the city of Sabratha. Sabratha was a Roman city located near Tunisia. When the missionaries arrived, the city of Sabratha was abandoned. Near the abandoned city were many Bantu villages. The villages were also abandoned. The Bantu had migrated south.

The missionaries found many carvings of a ram's head in the abandoned Bantu villages. The ram's head was unlike any ram found in Africa. The ram's head was like the ram found in Scandinavia. It was the image of a ram once used by the Germanic tribe of the Heruli. The Bantu worshiped the ram's head. It was called "Beberu Munga" - Ram of God.

The ram's head was a symbol of God's power. The ram's head was a symbol of God's love.

According to the Bantu legend, the Bantu lived near the sea in the land now known as Libya. The Bantu farmed the land and caught fish from the sea. The Bantu were peaceful people. Then, many warriors came to their land. The warriors captured young men, women, and children. The Bantu were taken to ships where they were to be sold into slavery.

The Bantu were powerless to stop the warriors. The Bantu prayed to God to help them and God heard their prayers.

God sent a great ram to Africa. On the back of the ram, clinging to its hair, were many fierce warriors.

The Ram of God

Also, clinging to the hair of the ram was a child healer - "Mwana Poza". When the great ram neared the Bantu villages, the Mwana Poza leaped from the ram. God sent the Mwana Poza to them and God sent the fierce warriors to free the captured Bantu.

The Beberu Munga ran on the sea searching for captive Bantu. The Beberu Munga would call out to the captured Bantu. When the captured Bantu heard the cry of the Beberu Munga, they would call out. The Beberu Munga would come to them. The fierce warriors would battle the slave warriors to free the captured Bantu. The captured Bantu would leap to the Beberu Munga and cling to its hair. The Beberu Munga would bring the captured Bantu to safety and freedom.

The Mwana Poza waited for the warriors and the Bantu to return. Many times, the warriors were injured in battle and the captive Bantu were ill. God healed the injured warriors and the ill Bantu through the hands of the Mwana Poza. One time, two of the warriors were killed in battle.

Two Bantu warriors were chosen to replace the two slain warriors.

The two Bantu warriors leapt to the Beberu Munga and they clung to its hair. The Beberu Munga ran on the sea to free captured Bantu slaves. The two Bantu warriors battled with God's warriors to free captured Bantu men, women, and children.

One day, the Beberu Munga returned. There were no captured Bantu slaves. The warriors of the slave ships were afraid to capture slaves. The Beberu Munga's task was complete. The Bantu were free and safe.

The Ram of God

The two Bantu warriors leapt from the Beberu Munga to the Bantu villages. The Beberu Munga and the warriors returned to heaven.

The Ram of God

The Bantu legend of the "Mwana Poza"

There are many stories of the Mwana Poza. The legends tell of several Mwana Pozas. The first Mwana Poza was a Bantu mtumwa - *child slave*. God sent a great warrior to free the mtumwa and God gave a great gift to the mtumwa. God healed through the hands of the mtumwa. God sent the Mwana Poza to the Bantu on the back of a great ram.

One story tells of many animals ill from drinking poisoned water. The animals called out to God. God sent the Mwana Poza to them. The Mwana Poza touched each animal and God healed the animals. Then, the Mwana Poza touched the poisoned water. God healed the water

God blessed the water. All animals came to drink from it without fear. The lion and the antelope drank together. Many Bantu went to the Water of Peace. They drank from the water with the lion.

One story tells of how God protected the Mwana Poza. God destroyed all that sought to harm the Mwana Poza by burning them in fire. The fire came from heaven.

One story tells of the Mwana Poza traveling to many Bantu villages. Behind the Mwana Poza, many thousands of Bantu followed. The Bantu followed the Mwana Poza to learn of God.

The Bantu followed the Mwana Poza to the land now known as Southern Africa.

The Ram of God

Appendix
The Children

Child's Name	Year C.E.	Gender /Race / Country
Rebecca	37	Girl/Hebrew
Aaron	44	Boy/Hebrew
Jessie	51	Boy/Hebrew
Hannah	58	Girl/Hebrew
Helsa	65	Girl/Hebrew
Semira	72	Girl/Hebrew
Avisha	79	Boy/Hebrew
Yahoash	86	Boy/Hebrew
Berakhiah	93	Boy/Hebrew
Jensine	100	Girl/Hebrew
Elhanan	107	Boy/Hebrew
Azaryahu	114	Boy/Hebrew
Manuela	121	Girl/Hebrew
Avidan	128	Boy/Hebrew
Elora	135	Girl/Hebrew
Abisha	142	Girl/Hebrew
Joachim	149	Boy/Hebrew
Zaneta	156	Girl/Hebrew
Raphael	163	Boy/Hebrew
Zedekiah	170	Boy/Hebrew
Hadar	177	Boy/Hebrew
Rafela	184	Girl/Hebrew
Taneli	191	Boy/Hebrew
Zadok	198	Boy/Hebrew
Aryeh	205	Boy/Hebrew
Malachy	212	Boy/Hebrew
Abiel	219	Boy/Hebrew
Beathag	226	Girl/Hebrew
Muslim	233	Boy/Egypt
Sadiki	240	Boy/Egypt
Halima	247	Girl/Egypt
Lateef	254	Boy/Egypt

The Ram of God

Child's Name	Year C.E.	Gender /Race / Country
Yahya	261	Boy/Egypt
Osahar	268	Boy/Egypt
Hakizimana	275	Boy/Egypt
Hasina	282	Girl/Egypt
Tumaini	289	Boy/Egypt
Eshe	296	Girl/Egypt
Yaminah	303	Girl/Egypt
Quibilah	310	Girl/Egypt
Chike	317	Boy/Egypt
Asim	324	Boy/Egypt
Nathifa	331	Girl/Egypt
Rashida	338	Girl/Egypt
Rashida	345	Girl/Egypt
Talibah	352	Girl/Egypt
Mandisa	359	Girl/Egypt
Jendayi	366	Girl/Egypt
Apophis	373	Boy/Egypt
Shani	380	Girl/Egypt
Agafia	387	Girl/Greece
Alena	394	Girl/Greece
Theon	401	Boy/Greece
Risto	408	Boy/Greece
Aretina	415	Girl/Greece
Cassie	422	Girl/Greece
Panteleimon	429	Boy/Greece
Lysander	436	Boy/Greece
Colette	443	Girl/Greece
Takis	450	Boy/Greece
Urian	457	Boy/Greece
Yalena	464	Girl/Greece
Theophilia	471	Girl/Greece
Habib	478	Boy/Africa
Iverem	485	Girl/Africa
Sisay	492	Girl/Africa
Basel	499	Boy/Africa
Akello	506	Boy/Africa
Abrihet	513	Girl/Africa

The Ram of God

Child's Name	Year C.E.	Gender / Race / Country
Iskinder	520	Boy/Africa
Armani	527	Girl/Africa
Diara	534	Boy/Africa
Mariama	541	Girl/Africa
Chinaka	548	Girl/Africa
Adom	555	Boy/Africa
Jaja	562	Boy/Africa
Yohance	569	Boy/Africa
Uchechi	576	Boy/Africa
Uchenna	583	Girl/Africa
Zuwena	590	Girl/Africa
Berhanu	597	Boy/Africa
Desta	604	Boy/Africa
Anaya	611	Girl/Africa
Erasto	618	Boy/Africa
Tamirat	625	Boy/Africa
Sadio	632	Girl/Africa
Asabi	639	Girl/Africa
Amari	646	Boy/Africa
Ghedi	653	Boy/Africa
Amachi	660	Girl/Africa
Bab-EL-Sama	667	Girl/Arabia
Damaa	674	Girl/Arabia
Taleb	681	Boy/Arabia
Majeed	688	Boy/Arabia
Al-Hadiye	695	Boy/Arabia
Ferhan	702	Boy/Arabia
Yasmeen	709	Girl/Arabia
Mahfouz	716	Boy/Arabia
Pavaka	723	Boy/India
Agastya	730	Boy/India
Anasuya	737	Girl/India
Kailasa	744	Girl/India
Shakra	751	Girl/India
Deven	758	Boy/India
Kabir	765	Boy/India
Bhagwandas	772	Boy/India

The Ram of God

Child's Name	Year C.E.	Gender / Race / Country
Sevti	779	Girl/India
Sitara	786	Girl/India
Yasmine	793	Girl/India
Kirati	800	Girl/India
Fai	807	Boy/China
Liang	814	Boy/China
Na	821	Girl/China
An	827	Girl/China
Tao	834	Girl/China
Shen	841	Boy/China
Jun	848	Girl/China
Wei	855	Girl/China
Chen	862	Boy/China
Cong	869	Boy/China
Lian	876	Boy/China
Ping	883	Girl/China
Shaiming	890	Boy/China
Sying	897	Boy/China
Yan Yan	904	Girl/China
Yu Jie	911	Girl/China
Zhen	918	Girl/China
Long	925	Boy/China
Hoshiko	932	Boy/China
Li	939	Boy/China
Nyoko	946	Girl/Japan
Hiroshi	953	Boy/Japan
Shika	960	Girl/Japan
Yoshi	967	Boy/Japan
Kioko	974	Girl/Japan
Koto	981	Girl/Japan
Michio	988	Boy/Japan
Naoko	995	Girl/Japan
Renjiro	1002	Boy/Japan
Jomei	1009	Boy/Japan
Suki	1016	Girl/Japan
Yuki	1023	Boy/Japan
Kaede	1030	Girl/Japan

The Ram of God

Child's Name	Year C.E.	Gender / Race / Country
Kyoto	1037	Girl/Japan
Chika	1044	Girl/Japan
Benjiro	1051	Boy/Japan
Kyoshi	1058	Boy/Japan
Kei	1065	Girl/Japan
Takeo	1072	Boy/Japan
Miya	1078	Girl/Japan
Shina	1085	Girl/Japan
Nami	1092	Girl/Japan
Sakura	1099	Girl/Japan
Kado	1106	Boy/Japan
Tamiko	1113	Girl/Japan
Dasha	1120	Girl/Russia
Yasha	1127	Boy/Russia
Fyodor	1134	Boy/Russia
Duscha	1141	Boy/Russia
Feodora	1148	Boy/Russia
Danya	1154	Boy/Russia
Semyon	1161	Boy/Russia
Ioakim	1168	Boy/Russia
Anna	1175	Boy/Russia
Vanya	1182	Girl/Russia
Elga	1189	Girl/Russia
Oleg	1196	Boy/Russia
Jelena	1203	Girl/Russia
Lubmilla	1210	Boy/Russia
Karina	1217	Boy/Russia
Staya	1224	Boy/Russia
Edik	1231	Boy/Russia
Yoana	1238	Girl/Spain
Alazne	1245	Girl/Spain
Amadeo	1252	Boy/Spain
Noe	1259	Boy/Spain
Mateo	1266	Boy/Spain
Benita	1273	Girl/Spain
Jose	1280	Boy/Spain
Casimiro	1287	Boy/Spain

The Ram of God

Child's Name	Year C.E.	Gender / Race / Country
Jesus	1294	Boy/Spain
Casta	1301	Girl/Spain
Sancia	1308	Girl/Spain
Raul	1315	Boy/Spain
Tobias	1322	Boy/Spain
Esperanza	1329	Girl/Spain
Helga	1336	Girl/Germany
Johanna	1343	Girl/Germany
Selik	1350	Boy/Germany
Oswald	1357	Boy/Germany
Wilhelm	1364	Boy/Germany
Engleberta	1371	Girl/Germany
Amara	1378	Girl/Germany
Maria	1385	Girl/England
Rebecca	1392	Girl/England
Victoria	1399	Girl/England
Eric	1406	Boy/England
Edward	1413	Boy/England
Raymond	1420	Boy/England
Ronald	1427	Boy/England
Annabelle	1434	Girl/England
Bruce	1441	Boy/England
Catherine	1448	Girl/England
Grace	1455	Girl/England
Michelle	1462	Girl/England
Valerie	1469	Girl/England
Elizabeth	1476	Girl/England
Ruth	1483	Girl/England
Michael	1490	Boy/England
Paul	1497	Boy/England
Rachel	1504	Girl/England
Samuel	1511	Boy/England
Winston	1518	Boy/England
Charles	1525	Boy/England
Harris	1532	Boy/England
Robert	1539	Boy/England
Suzanne	1546	Girl/England

The Ram of God

Child's Name	Year C.E.	Gender / Race / Country
Mary	1553	Girl/England
Timothy	1560	Boy/England
Eirica	1567	Girl/Scotland
Leana	1574	Girl/Scotland
Tyra	1581	Girl/Scotland
Ronald	1588	Boy/Scotland
Bonnie	1595	Girl/Scotland
Macrae	1602	Boy/Scotland
Wallace	1609	Boy/Scotland
Carmichael	1616	Boy/Scotland
Christel	1623	Girl/Scotland
Isobel	1630	Girl/Scotland
Malcolm	1637	Boy/Scotland
Iain	1644	Boy/Scotland
Jean	1651	Girl/Scotland
Morrison	1658	Boy/Scotland
Parlan	1665	Boy/Scotland
Siubhan	1672	Girl/Scotland
Sinclair	1679	Boy/Scotland
Ailbert	1686	Boy/Scotland
Mackay	1693	Boy/Scotland
Brianna	1700	Girl/Ireland
Colmcilla	1707	Girl/Ireland
Fineena	1714	Girl/Ireland
Tullia	1721	Girl/Ireland
Seafraid	1728	Boy/Ireland
Malone	1735	Boy/Ireland
Terrence	1742	Boy/Ireland
Patrick	1749	Boy/Ireland
Aideen	1756	Girl/Ireland
Brian	1763	Boy/Ireland
Cristin	1770	Girl/Ireland
Eamon	1777	Boy/Ireland
Eveleen	1784	Girl/Ireland
Kathleen	1791	Girl/Ireland
Keegan	1798	Boy/Ireland
Moreen	1805	Girl/Ireland

The Ram of God

Child's Name	Year C.E.	Gender / Race / Country
Nolan	1812	Boy/Ireland
Quinlan	1819	Boy/Ireland
Whelan	1826	Boy/Ireland
Aengus	1833	Boy/Ireland
Eilis	1840	Girl/Ireland
Gilchrist	1847	Boy/Ireland
Godfrey	1854	Boy/Ireland
Jeoffroi	1861	Boy/France
Mahieu	1868	Boy/France
Esperanza	1875	Girl/France
Amedee	1882	Girl/France
Rene	1889	Boy/France
Elitta	1896	Girl/France
Sennet	1903	Boy/France
Cateline	1910	Girl/France
Benedetta	1917	Girl/Italy
Donato	1924	Boy/Italy
Matteo	1931	Boy/Italy
Agnella	1938	Girl/Italy
Giovanni	1945	Boy/Italy
Leonora	1952	Girl/Italy
Teodora	1959	Girl/Italy
Renata	1966	Girl/Italy
Maceo	1973	Boy/Italy
Amadeo	1980	Boy/Italy
Antonio	1987	Boy/Italy
Elizabeth	1994	Girl/America
Samuel *	2001	Boy/America

* Samuel was born in America. Samuel is of African decent.

The Author

Edward Ronny Arnold may have created the first electronic book. In 1984, he created a stand-alone computer program, which allowed a person to read the story in one of eight reading speeds. The story he created was titled, *The Story of Creation. The Story of Creation* is the computerized version of the first chapters of Genesis from the King James Version of the Holy Bible.

In 1989, Edward created the first electronic newspaper, *News Disk* ®. *News Disk* ® contained animation, real photographs, sound effects, and voice. The February 1990 issue, dedicated to Black History Month, included portions of a speech by Dr. Martin Luther King, Jr. The speech was the actual voice of Dr. Martin Luther King, Jr.

Edward's software programs have been nominated for several awards. Among the nominations are: *Number Cross*™, *Aesop's Fables - The Hare and the Tortoise*, and *News Disk* ®.

The Ram of God

The Ram of God © is Edward's fourth original novel. Edward holds the degrees of BS in Psychology and the MA in Sociology from Middle Tennessee State University. Edward resides in Nashville, Tennessee with his wife, Michelle, and their daughter, Khristine.

The Ram of God © is published as an electronic book on the **Computer Classics** ® website.

The Ram of God © is a book, which will be read for many years.

Fall 2001

Rebecca
A Journey of Man

And the great healer passed his hand over the child and a third time he held up the child for all to see. And a third time he spoke to the crowd saying, "It is the will of God that for generations to come all with know the power of God through the hands of a child. What was given to me has been given to her. This child is protected by God himself. No man, woman, child, or beast of the earth shall harm this child. This is the will of God."

And the great healer handed the child to her parents and he touched them and he blessed them. And he spoke to them saying, "Your child will serve God. Return to your place and share the blessing which God has given."

The Apostle Simon Peter spoke these words in the year 37 CE. With these words, a journey began.

This is a journey that will take you from the gates of the city of Jerusalem to the mountains of Asia.

This is a journey that will take you from the battlefields of World War II to the playhouse of three young children.

The Ram of God

This is a journey of love and compassion. This is a journey of hope and forgiveness. This is a journey, which is not complete.

Rebecca was selected as one of the first books highlighted in the First Annual Celebration of Inspirational Authors held in conjunction with the Southern Festival of Books - Fall 2002.

Rebecca was one of five finalists for the 2003 Eppie Award for Best Inspirational Book.

Published Books

The Lepers

*God gives to each our needs. God does not
give more. God does not give less.*

The lepers traveled to Jerusalem to welcome Jesus
Christ into the city. When they arrived, Jesus had
been crucified and buried.

The lepers would not abandon God. The lepers would
not abandon Jesus. The people of Jerusalem drove
them from the city with stones. The lepers would not
leave. They waited at the gates of Jerusalem. They
waited for the disciples of Jesus.

The people of Jerusalem cursed them. The people of
Jerusalem spat upon them. The people of Jerusalem
laughed at them. The Commander of the Roman
soldiers threatened them.

The lepers would not leave. They would not abandon
God. They would not abandon Jesus. They waited at
the gates of Jerusalem. They waited for the disciples
of Jesus.

And as they waited, their numbers increased.

The Lepers is a powerful story of the faith of the
outcast.

The Ram of God

Published Books

Rashida

The greatest illness of man is not of the body, it is of the spirit

In the year 338 CE, invaders sought to conquer Egypt. Their goal was simple, destroy every Christian. Destroy their temples and their monuments. Murder every man, women, and child.

One man stood in their way, Tarik. Tarik and his soldiers battled the invaders with courage and cunning.

Tarik had less than four hundred soldiers. The invaders are many thousands. Tarik and his soldiers could not defeat their numbers; they defeated their spirit.

In a climactic battle, Tarik and his soldiers battle many thousands of the invaders. The invaders quickly and easily defeat Tarik and his soldiers.

The invaders stand poised to invade Egypt. Many thousands of the invaders stand before the home of Tarik and within Tarik's home are many Christians. Within Tarik's home is Rashida.

The invaders have one left to battle. Only one stands in their way to murder every man, woman, and child in Egypt. Only one defends Egypt. Only one protects the families and the homes.

The one is Rashida's protector.

The Ram of God

Upcoming Books

Spring 2004

The Tenth Scroll – The book everyone is waiting for. Who wrote the tenth scroll? What does it say? Why did Titus not reveal the scroll? All of your questions will be answered. *The Tenth Scroll* has already been written. It is scheduled for release in the spring of 2004.

Spring 2008

Samuel – In the year 2001, God took the gift from Elizabeth and gave the gift to Samuel. In the year 2008, Samuel will pass the gift to another. Who is Samuel? What has happened in Samuel's life? The story of Samuel does not begin in the year 2001. The story of Samuel begins in the year 478. Descendents of Samuel are captured in Africa and taken to Greece to be sold as slaves. God sends the angel Jaykal to return the captured people to their home. This is an exciting book that traces the descendents of Samuel from the continent of Africa to the Civil Rights movement in the 1960's. Samuel is descended from Habib.

No Date Given

El-Mabka – the Place of Weeping – "A young child will pass the gift to another. And God will perform great feats of healing through the hands of the child. And all will be made known of the child. And all will know of God's power through the hands of the child. And many will come unto God and the Christ through the child." This is the final book related to *Rebecca*. *El-Mabka – the Place of Weeping* has already been written. No date of publication has been given.

The Ram of God

The Ram of God

The Ram of God

The Ram of God

The Ram of God